BE GOOD YOUR LIFE DEPENDS ON IT

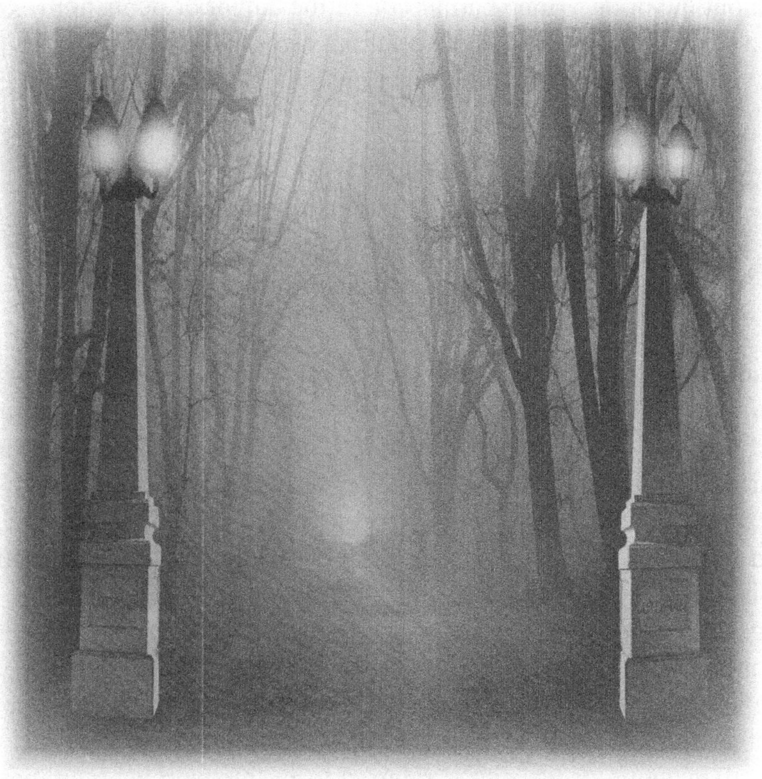

Savanna Loy

ReSet: Be Good Your Life Depends On It
Savanna Loy

ISBN: 978-1-956193-26-8
Book Design & Publishing done by:
Global Book Publishing
www.globalbookpublishing.com

DEDICATION

There is an endless list with names on it to whom I could dedicate this book to. God, my family, friends, supporters, etc. However, for this book I want to specifically mention my biological father, who is no longer with me. You see, he was hit by a drunk driver before I was born and all he ever wanted was a little girl named Savanna.

He got that, but my parents divorced when I was two. I never got the chance to really be around him much and when I did, he was a stranger, but we both loved each other. His circumstances didn't allow him to be what he wanted to be. More than anything he wanted to help me achieve my dreams, but didn't know how. Sadly, he passed away two years ago, but when he did, he left me all he had. It wasn't much, but it was enough to reach a HUGE dream of mine. To be an author. This book, has his love wrapped up in my dream. Thanks Dad. Until we meet again.

Your little Savanna

PROLOGUE

Wait, I need to catch my breath. I'm not as young as I used to be, Sal.

"I'm older than you, Mick. We just got started. I'm not surprised you can't keep up with Lightning Sal, but this is sad, even for you."

"Watch it, sir. I can still whup your butt."

"Okay, okay. I'll slow down, bud. They don't make 'em like they used to in my day, I guess. We're almost to the park entrance. We'll stop at the lamp posts this time, but I hope you'll be able to handle this run tomorrow. You know how important these are to me."

"Yeah, I know. Sorry, Sal. Tomorrow will be better. I think it was the wife's chimichangas. They're catching up to me," Mick explained as a burp escaped his lips.

Sal looked at Mick in disgust. "Come on, man. Let's not make things worse," he teased.

Maintaining a leisurely pace, the men continued down the pathway. The offbeat thuds of their footsteps paired with Mick's heavy breathing was all that could be heard. The sickening silence around them was a reminder of the reality of what their lives had become. This caused Mick to ponder the park and what it used to look like before the ReSet. Typically, during these runs, Mick and Sal would keep to casual conversation and childlike banter to occupy their time. However, with Mick barely able to breathe, that wasn't on the agenda this evening. Unfortunately, this left him to his thoughts. He pictured kids playing with their families and assumed there had been genuine happiness then. Now, he could tell the parents tried to fake it, but their true happiness was buried beneath the constant fear of the looming threat. Their town had done well for the first five years and had seemed to get the hang of it, but the new addition over the last four years made him uneasy. He was terrified they wouldn't make it to the next ReFresh, despite it being a mere three months away. Truthfully, he was worried they wouldn't last another three days.

Sal kept looking back checking on Mick. He knew that their marathon training was pointless now, but their nightly runs together somehow made him feel normal. True, the world had turned dark, but he didn't think it deserved what it got. He was desperate for the life he had before, but this was the best he could get. He was sad Mick needed to stop already, but at least the wife would be surprised by his early return home.

Mick could barely catch his breath. "Okay, Sal. I see the posts. Let's call it. I seriously feel like my lungs are about to explode!"

Sal dropped back in line with his buddy. "Mick, you call yourself a soldier. Man up, let's finish this."

Sal knew what buttons to push, and he did it on purpose. This caused Mick to pick up his pace. There was no way he was going to let his friend get away with that comment. They were always competing in basic training, and this was going to be no different. Although Sal always beat him in a foot race, Mick wasn't going down without a fight. Sal, excited his prodding worked, increased his speed as well.

Both lamp posts were in sight now. These lamp posts were no doubt custom-made and were integral to this city's original design. They had stood the test of time, but you could tell that mother nature had won a few battles. Each crack, rivet, and missing chunk of concrete held a story. They towered around twenty feet with intricately designed square bases as wide as a small car. The bases were paired with concrete columns that got smaller as they reached into the sky. Atop the smallest part of the columns were two separate glass lamp heads, gothic in design. Seeming to float above the path, the warm yellow light didn't provide much visibility but rather gave off an eerie glow that almost served as a warning to keep out. The bottom of each base was adorned with a metal sign that had been added upon the city's first milestone four and a half years ago and it simply said, "UTOPIAN: SOMEONE IS ALWAYS WATCHING." It sent a shiver down Mick's spine every time he read it. Its words were simple and to the point. He knew it wasn't an empty threat. The plaque's contrast to the post's authentic design was intentional—to remind the citizens that a change had been put in place and they had no business trying to go backward.

Excited about his easy victory, Sal wanted to really rub it in. "Ha, I beat you, youngin."

Although he had lost, Mick took pleasure in the fact that Sal's breathing had, too, accelerated, his words barely squeaking out. "Looks like you're aging as well," said Mick and flashed him a smile, still panting.

Sal's grin spread across his face as he lifted his hands above his head to catch his breath. Both men began stretching, using the bases to maintain balance. When their cool-down had ended and they started heading back, it happened. The sound they had been dreading for the past nine years rang so loud that the men simultaneously grabbed their ears. They both went pale as ghosts as they looked at each other. Even in the midst of war, Sal had never seen such fear in his friend's eyes. Mick had always been so jovial, but now, his eyes were dead.

Sal cupped Mick's face. "Mick, focus. This isn't a drill. This is it."

Mick shook his head, ran to the edge of the path, and threw up. It couldn't be. He wasn't home. He wasn't with his family. "I have to go ... to go ... to get Trish and Steven. They need me," Mick stuttered.

"No, you don't. You have to stick to the plan. You know we don't have a choice," Sal said.

Mick shook his head again. He was their protector. There was no way he was leaving Trish to do this alone. He knew she had to be freaking out at the house. He had to get back. He began to take off but felt a jolt as Sal pulled him back by his shirt. Sal turned him around and looked him dead in the eyes.

"I mean it, Mick. Think clearly. This is what we've been training for these past several months. We're out of time. Stick to the plan," Sal said. He was equally scared, but Mick was like a little brother. He had always looked out for him, and he wasn't going to stop now. As if the lamp posts were listening in on the conversation and waiting to make their grand reveal, the ground began to tremble around them. Both men watched, knowing what would happen next. They had seen the plans and the simulations, but this was the first time they would witness it in action. The center of the post began to divide, slowly opening up. If it wasn't for the reason they were doing this, both men would have been in total awe. The sound of the post splitting in addition to the city alarm blaring was deafening. Sal tried to say something to Mick, but he was unable to hear it. The post finally stopped moving, and Sal yelled for Mick to get in. Sal ran to the post, reached inside, and jumped without hesitation, disappearing right before Mick's eyes. Mick swallowed hard. He had always prayed it wouldn't come to this. He ran to the entrance now created by the post and reached inside. He felt the cold hard metal in his hands. He knew he had found the interior pole that he himself had helped build. He took a deep breath and closed his eyes. He was always nervous about the jump. Practicing at the fire station suddenly didn't seem like enough. He also knew there would be no mat to catch him at the end of this ten-foot drop. He looked around at the empty dark park and could feel his own emptiness inside him surfacing. He was trying not to get emotional. This town had been home for nine years, and although he absolutely loathed the reason he was there, his family had created memories in this place. His heart ached. "Please make it, Trish," he whispered out loud, then swallowed again and jumped.

DESOLATION

I don't like it here, Father. When can we leave? asked Katie.

Her father and mother hadn't told her where they were going. They never got to leave the city, and she was very excited. You had to have special permission to leave, and the entire trip, she had wondered about what great things her family would do. Pulling up to this city was not what she had expected. It had taken six hours, and the destination didn't seem worth the trip. She had hesitated even getting out of the car, but she knew better than to disobey.

"Soon, K.K., soon. This is very important, and I need you both to pay close attention," he said as he grabbed Katie's hand and kissed the top of it.

This made her smile and immediately melted the worry that had just engulfed her. She loved her father very much and although she was ready to leave, she knew if her father had brought her family to this creepy, abandoned city, he had to have a reason. She had learned at a very young age that she could always trust him. She was now thirteen, and her trust in him hadn't waivered. She knew, growing up, that life didn't seem quite normal, but her father had always made their family seem normal.

She had a beautiful mother and a brother who took great care of her. They never argued or fought. Life in her city had seemed perfect while she was growing up, but she couldn't help shake the feeling that was what made it not seem real. Her happy bubble had popped after the Tankersons arrived. Their beloved city was in bad shape, and she could feel her father's stress each night. He tried to put on a brave front, but she knew her father. As they continued walking down the deserted street, passing empty building after empty building, a memory flashed into her mind. There were two men in suits that had shown up at their house when they first moved there. Her mother was at the store, and she was in the living room playing with her brother, Charlie. Her father had told Charlie to take her to her room and stay there. Charlie was four years older than Katie and had always been very protective. He did exactly as her father had asked without hesitation. They hadn't been in the room for very long when they heard screaming, both from the men and their father. Katie had never even heard her father raise his voice, and this immediately worried her. She also remembered the fear in Charlie's eyes, and it made her start to cry. She was so young, and she had no idea what was going on, but she did remember Charlie taking her into the closet and holding her ears so she couldn't hear the yelling. She remembered feeling so scared, much like the way she did now. She had never told her father she remembered that night. She was afraid he wouldn't want to talk to her about it, but a part of her was also afraid he would. She shook the memory from her mind and tuned back into the lecture her father was giving. It wasn't the first time she had heard this; she could practically give it herself. She didn't mind, though. Her father's voice was soothing. It echoed through the desolate streets and over the abandoned buildings and back to them. It was rough yet kind, and the idea that it was surrounding them in a city where everyone had completely vanished brought Katie a certain reassurance that she didn't even realize she needed until that moment.

"Say, it with me, kids. Remember the ReSetter motto," Father said.

"Be good; someone is always watching," the family rang in unison.

They had said this motto their entire lives. They were made to say it to begin their school days and each night as they got ready for bed. It wasn't just the ReSetter motto; it had become their own.

"Very good, very good," Father replied.

They walked on further ahead in silence. Mother and Father kept exchanging looks, but Katie couldn't tell what they were trying to say. They had always been able to silently communicate. She figured it was just what husbands and wives did, but Charlie had said that they were special. He said they were each other's everything and knew exactly what was on each other's minds at exactly the same time. Katie often dreamed about what her husband would be like, and she wanted a love just like her parents. Sadly though, the world she was growing up in didn't give her hope that she would ever find something as special as what her parents had. Because of Tommy Tankerson, she was wondering if she would even make it to her fourteenth birthday. Her mother had told her not to think in that way, but she couldn't help it. She had tried to talk to Tommy about his behavior, and he seemed to listen, but when Charlie approached them, Tommy shut down and walked away. She hated herself for thinking he was so cute.

She returned to her father's lecture once again. He was at the part where he was explaining how this ReSet city didn't make it to their first ReFresh, let alone their first year. He was re-explaining Grayson's decision that was currently impacting their lives.

"So, we're here for you to teach us a lesson?" Katie asked.

Father smiled and paused. "Not exactly, K.K. We're here to show you what happened because of people not behaving."

Charlie was careful not to roll his eyes. He found it amazing that his father wasn't placing the blame exactly where it belonged. His father had said that he had gotten permission to turn their chips off, but he never fully trusted Grayson, a secret he had kept to himself his entire life.

"We have a very important job to do in our city, and we have to set the example. We don't want to end up like this town. We can't go back to the way the world was; we must create a better future. But the ReSetters are watching, and it's important that we do things correctly. It's important that you guys help me with Tommy. This is just a friendly reminder to the two of you. Our family is so important to our city."

Mother gave Katie a reassuring squeeze on the shoulder as they continued walking. The emptiness of the town was enough of a lesson, even without Father's explanation. Although father had said it had been less than a year that this town had gone through a full ReSet, it seemed as if it had been centuries. She knew each key city was selected for its remoteness, but this town seemed uncomfortably isolated. She wondered how much restoration had been done before they started "the new beginning". She could see char marks on some of the buildings while other buildings looked incomplete. She wondered at which time of destruction these scars on the buildings had been made. As they turned down another street, something caught Katie's attention, instantly bringing tears to her eyes. There was a pink tricycle knocked over near a blue and white house. Ivy had grown around the tires. There were only a few glittery ribbons left on the handlebars, and the white basket on the front of the bike was barely hanging on. She pictured a blonde-haired little girl with two perfect curled pigtails with ribbons perfectly matching her dress, squealing with laughter, no doubt feeling like she could take on the world, pedaling that bike. She knew that this had once been a prized possession to some little girl. Now it was left abandoned just like the city. Some little girl had not only lost her bike but her life, and Katie couldn't shake the desolate feeling it gave her. She had been indoctrinated about Alpha and the ReSetters and all the history behind it in school and at home. It always seemed to make sense and seem reasonable when it was taught to her, but she couldn't shake the feeling of despair she now felt seeing this city firsthand. She knew what had happened here, and she couldn't understand how it could be okay. She knew better than to share any of this with anyone. It would have serious repercussions. Her heart also sank for Bo.

A loud bang halted the family's walk and thoughts. Father held up his hand to stop them. He looked at mother, who shook her head as if he had given her a command. Mother took Katie by the hand, stepping in front of her. She then took Charlie and put him behind Father. Father reached his hand behind him and rested it on something lumpy under his coat. Katie hadn't noticed it before and was curious as to what it was. Another bang made Charlie jump. Father took two steps forward and looked back at Mother. Without hesitation, she grabbed both children and hurried them to a nearby business. The broken glass still littered the entranceway. Mother carefully stepped over the remaining shards on the bottom of the door and stepped inside. She motioned for both children to do the same thing. They followed suit and waited inside the empty business.

"What is this place?" Katie whispered.

"Didn't you read the door? It said Buster's Barbershop," Charlie replied.

Katie looked around and noticed the lonely chair in the middle of the shop. Its burgundy leather had been faded by the sun and it had ripped in more than one place with the foam cushion beneath the leather emerging. The supplies that she assumed had once been neatly arranged on the counter were scattered everywhere. Pictures on the wall had been knocked down. She pictured the employees and customers on their peak days. She wanted to believe this was a place where happiness was shared. She wanted to believe that this was a place where there wasn't always a feeling of sadness ready to overtake you. She pictured men getting fresh shaves with hot towels and women with curlers in their hair. Thinking of this ReSet city made her go further in her imagination to what the original city had looked like before the mass ReSet. Mother had warned her not to talk to people about it, but she couldn't help but dream about it. She shook the image from her head and then begin to wonder what was taking Father so long.

"Nobody's supposed to be here, Mother. This is a ReSet city. I want Father to come back," Charlie said.

"You're right, Charlie. Nobody should be here, which is exactly why we are going to hide until we know it's safe," Mother replied.

Charlie shook his head. He knew better than to argue with his mother. It was one of the many rules he knew he had to follow. He didn't want to end up like this city. An eruption of laughter made all three of them jump in unison. Katie immediately recognized it. Her Father's boisterous laughter always stood out in a crowd. It was infectious, and usually, it didn't take long for the rest of the family to join in. However, they had no idea why he was laughing, and curiosity, not laughter was over taking them.

"Alford Newsome," Mother said as she stepped out of her hiding space and back into the street, "You had better tell me, this instant, what in the world is going on."

"I'm sorry, Mother," Father replied. "It's safe to come out. I found the big bad scary noise," he said with a chuckle.

Mother joined him in his laughter with her own delicate giggle. Sometimes you couldn't even tell she was laughing because it was so faint. However, one way you always knew she was laughing was by the twinkle in her deep green eyes. She motioned for both children to come out. As they joined her in the street, they both started snickering as well. Father was holding a small dog. He was covered in mud and what appeared to be fleas. Despite the thick mud, you could see a few spots of white fur. He had one black patch of fur on his tail.

"I found this little guy in the bottom of a metal trash can," Father explained. "I guess he was looking for food and fell into it. Lucky for him, we were in this city, or he too would have been like the rest of the folks here."

"How do you suppose he got here, Al?" Mother asked.

"I have no idea," Father replied. He patted the dog on the head. "He needs a good bath, though."

Katie's eyes filled with excitement, and she jumped up and down. "Does this mean we're going to keep him?"

Katie could see the worry on Mother's face. "We can't, Al. I don't know if the head chair would approve," Mother said.

"Well, I don't think they would approve of us leaving him out here to die. That's not the right thing to do," Father replied.

"Listen to what you just said. It's exactly what they do," Mother responded.

"Touché," Father said. "I'm afraid you're right, Mother. It pains me to say, but we're going to have to leave him here."

He met his family's gaze and saw their sadness. The sight almost instantly moved him to tears. He hated to see them this way, but he knew with the way things were right now back at Utopian, they really couldn't deal with any distractions, and Grayson didn't need any other reasons to go against them. As if to try to change his mind, the puppy began whimpering and licking his face. Charlie recognized that his father was struggling, and he wanted to try and help. He stepped to his father and patted the puppy on his head. He looked at his father and forced a smile. He pressed his forehead against the puppy's.

"We would have called you Nix," Charlie whispered. "It's really fine, Father. We're not upset at all."

He shot a glance at his sister, warning her to agree. She didn't respond but slowly nodded her head. "Come on K.K.," Charlie said. "Let's at least try to see if we can find him something to eat and build him a shelter." This seemed to bring a little light to Katie's face. She grabbed the puppy from her father, kissed the top of his head, and ran off in front of her brother.

As soon as the children were further down the road, Beth grabbed Father's hand. "There's something you aren't telling me, dear," she said.

"In due time," he replied.

The family found a place for the puppy and even found a few supplies scattered on the floor of the town's market. They all knew in their hearts that the dog probably wouldn't make it much longer, but they didn't want to focus on that. So, they headed back the way they had come, doing their best to shut out the whining behind them. Surroundings notwithstanding, it was a picture-perfect moment for this family. For a moment, it almost made them forget what the world had come to. They neared the car parked at the edge of the city sign, which was riddled with bullet holes. The original town name, Ravensburg, had been blacked out with spray paint and the new name, Phoenix, had been painted in its place. The plan had been to erect a new concrete sign upon the first ReFresh. It never made it. Father looked back one last time at the city before he got into the car. Unlike Katie and the rest of his family, he did remember what the original city looked like. He had helped to destroy it. Unlike his children, he also remembered what the world had been like. He had helped to destroy that world—a matter of necessity.

THE KINGS REVEALED

~ Chair #2

The drive back to Utopian was long and silent. The Newsome children had both fallen asleep, and since Mrs. Newsome had stopped scratching her husband's arm ten minutes ago, he knew it was just a matter of time before she, too, was asleep. He didn't mind. He needed to gather his thoughts and he knew the best way to do that was with the silence his family had created. He still had a few more plans to get together before he talked to his wife, Beth, about what he felt they now needed to do and what they needed to change. He looked over at her and confirmed she was indeed asleep. For the next several minutes, he stole glances at his slumbering spouse while maintaining control of the wheel. Not that it really mattered. The road was as deserted as it was long. He could have driven anywhere he wanted without the threat of hitting another vehicle. In the wake of the full ReSet, they rarely were seen at all. Citizens weren't allowed travel, let alone operate vehicles unless they belonged to the founding family of a key city. Since there were only four originally, and now just three, he wasn't concerned about running into anyone, or really anything on this lonesome road. It was yet another reminder of the terrible mistake he had made. Beth randomly twitched her nose in her sleep. She was self-conscious about it, even though he found it endearing. He reached over and tucked a strand of strawberry blonde hair that had fallen out of her messy bun behind her ear. She didn't even flinch. He caressed her cheek with the back of his hand. He adored the feel of her soft skin. He sighed deeply. He knew she would go along with the plan; she was always by his side. However, they had already had to change so much in their lives because of him. They had finally settled into this current life they were living. He knew his decision about changing things again was necessary. He wished he had never gone along with the plan, to begin with. The thought of all those people gone because of a choice he helped to make made him nauseous. He had to shake the thought from his mind just so he could maintain his composure. He looked back at Beth and remembered the first day of their new life. The day Utopian was founded...

***

"It's a perfect day, isn't it Alford?"

"David, is there a real reason that G.J. couldn't make it for this special occasion?"

David shifted in his seat, seemingly uneasy about the question. "You know how demanding it is to run Alpha. He wanted to be here. He said to send his regards. You were so instrumental in getting all this going, and he does wish he could be here," he replied.

Mr. Newsome shrugged his shoulders and kept typing. He had a few more lines of code to run, and then everything would be set. He didn't mind having Dave here for the big reveal, but it seemed strange that Grayson wouldn't have come himself. After all, it was the first city to be ReSet after the world's annihilation, and they had worked for several years to make sure everything would be perfect. You wouldn't miss the birth of your own child, and for both Alford Newsome and Grayson Jeffers, that was exactly what this felt like. Al looked back at Dave, spinning around in his chair. He had always admired David King's ability to turn even the most stressful situation into a lighthearted affair. However, right now he needed more silence to work and make sure they started on time. David had been instrumental in making sure all the health precautions were in place. He had gone ahead to each chosen city and made sure that there were zero health concerns that would prohibit them from being filled with the new citizens.

"Do you remember that day?" David asked, interrupting Al's thoughts.

"Which day, David? We've had a lot of new days these last several years." Alford answered.

"The day you met Grayson," David said as he stood up to look out the window. He could hear Al say something in response, but he was already mentally in another place. A place that brought both happiness and hurt at the very same time. A place he frequently visited.

David King was an oncologist with everything going for him. He and his wife had celebrated five years of marriage and were on top of the world. They had both agreed that two doctors getting married wouldn't provide the ideal environment to raise a child and ensure that they would be able to give their child the attention they felt he would need. They also had both agreed that they equally loved their jobs and weren't ready for either of them to quit. Neither of them had ever planned on marrying. Making it through medical school had taught them both that you can live without a social life, and they had come to understand that they were both happy with that decision. However, what they weren't planning on was that after David's transfer to a new hospital, their lives would forever be changed.

Maddison Parks was the chief of medicine at Rose City Memorial Hospital and had been paged to the upstairs breakroom for what had been referred to as a "situation". She had just started a double shift and was not in the mood. She hadn't been expecting to walk into what she did on the night she met David King. When she made it into the breakroom on the fourth floor, her jaw nearly hit the floor. There was a doctor standing with his back facing her on one of the tables, balancing an empty can on his head and trying to juggle plastic utensils from the cafeteria. Two other doctors were filming him with their phones, and their laughter was starting to become disruptive to the nursing staff. Maddison was appalled.

"Doctor, to my office now. You two, back on your floors," Maddison ordered.

She turned around without waiting to see if her employees complied. She knew they would. She continued walking down the hallway toward her office. She could hear the heavy footsteps behind her, and she could feel her anger rising. She had worked long and hard to turn this hospital around. It was finally being recognized as a place of professionalism in the city, and she couldn't believe that one of her staff was acting in that manner. Worst of all, it would now probably be on the 10 o'clock news, and she would be to blame. Although she passed several nurses on the way, nobody spoke to her. They knew better. She made it to her office, opened the door, stepped inside, and went straight to her chair.

"Do you have anything to say for yourself?" she asked as she began to sit down.

"Nice shoes," the doctor answered.

She looked up from where she had just sat down in utter disbelief, and then she finally saw him. His mysterious gray eyes caught her off guard, and she forgot for a moment what she was going to say. His sandy hair was a mess. It appeared the doctor apparently couldn't afford a comb. He had a goofy grin on his face that for some reason made her smirk. She tried to contain her smile. He also had dimples which were noticeable not only when he smiled but also when he spoke. She had always had a secret attraction to a man with dimples. The most unique thing about him, though, was his freckles. He had freckles across his face from cheek to cheek. She knew she hadn't met many men with a face full of freckles, but for this doctor, they fit his personality, and she couldn't believe that she actually found it attractive. Her cheeks blushed as she realized she was staring for too long. "Excuse me," she replied.

He had never really paid attention to his boss either and was surprised at her beauty. She had dark black hair which stood in stark contrast to her soft brown eyes. She seemed so put together, but something in her eyes seemed sad.

"Your shoes. I like them. It's not every day you see hot pink heels on a doctor," he explained.

Maddison was offended. "I'll have you know, I run this hospital; I'm not just a doctor. May I also remind you that I'm your boss? Who are you and why don't I recognize you? What's your name and your field?"

"David King. Oncology. Just started two weeks ago. I was hoping for more of a welcome, but I see it's not your style, Madi," he answered.

Maddison was infuriated. "That's Doctor Parks to you, Doctor King. I would expect a level of respect from you. I have no idea what you were thinking down there. Nor do I think you know how hard I've worked to establish this hospital and turn it around from where it was. I'm not sure what you're used to at your previous employment, but here at Rose City—"

"I lost one today," David interrupted. "I am sorry, but I was trying to take my mind off it, and I figured getting a few laughs from some colleagues would help."

Maddison stopped her lecture and remained silent.

"It was a patient that was already here when I transferred in. I started doing some new trials with him, and he seemed to be getting better. His wife cried on my shoulder and thanked me for giving him a second chance. However, his cancer had spread further than I was initially aware of, and there was no chance of him surviving ... and he died today. His wife spat in my face and said she would never forgive me for giving her false hope," David continued. He looked down to the floor and picked at his fingers. He often used humor to mask how he was feeling, but now he was afraid he may have taken it too far.

Maddison paused a few moments. She felt her heart break for this man, and it caught her off guard. She didn't even know him. Losing patients was part of their daily lives, so why did she feel so concerned about what this doctor was going through? "I see. I'm so sorry. I personally know how tough that is. Here at Rose City Memorial, we do have counselors on call twenty-four hours if you need to speak to someone. Although I can empathize with your reasoning as to why you chose those antics in the breakroom, I would ask that in the future, you choose a way to cope that doesn't potentially bring any unwanted attention to our hospital. With that being said, this will just be a verbal warning for now. If you need to take the rest of the shift to cope, then I will approve that. Is there anything you'd like to add?"

David opened his mouth to speak but paused. He watched Maddison for a moment. She was perfectly put together, but he couldn't shake the thought that there was something hiding beneath that perfection. He had never had anyone catch his attention the way she had, and she wasn't even trying. He had never felt this way before, and he was impulsive, so he wasn't shocked by his response. "You wanna go grab a coffee after our shift ends?"

That was the beginning for the two of them. Their romance was a whirlwind, and they only need forty-two days to know they belonged with each other. They had met late in life and decided they didn't want to put off another day, so they married in a very intimate service and never regretted it once.

Five years passed for them very quickly. They had built a house and taken many adventures. They had a list of a hundred places to see before they celebrated fifty years and they were on target to reach that goal—maybe sooner. Nothing could have prepared David King for what would be next. They were on one of their adventures, this time in Italy. Maddison hadn't been feeling well for several days. Her appetite had seemed to diminish, which wasn't like her. She was a sucker for carbs. She had figured it was jet lag. On their second morning there, a sharp pain in her stomach woke her up. It was so intense she was unable to go back to sleep. Her tears woke David, who was immediately alert. Both having medical backgrounds, they quickly went through the checklist. Maddison saw the fear in David's eyes. She wasn't quite sure what he had figured out. He assured her that they needed to get to a hospital quickly. He wouldn't tell her what he believed it to be. He said there was no need in stressing until they had results. Sadly, what he was afraid of was exactly what it was. Pancreatic cancer. His wife—the one he hadn't been looking for, the one who had changed him for the better, the one who had made waking up extra sweet—had pancreatic cancer, and he, the oncologist, could do nothing to help her. Her pancreas was riddled with it. They tried everything to fight it, but within a year, she was gone. He had failed as an oncologist, but more importantly, he had failed as her husband. The loss killed him too. He had never been quite the same. Rose City was legally his, but he couldn't stand walking down those halls let alone running the place. Yet, he knew Maddison would never forgive him if he sold it. He hired the best he could find to run it and then left to focus all his efforts and finances on finding a cure for cancer. He was ashamed he hadn't tried earlier in his career. Maybe if he had, his wife would still be alive.

It was the two-year anniversary of Maddison's death when Grayson Jeffers approached him. He had a lot of information on David King, and it was chilling to David to hear all of his secrets out in the open. Grayson Jeffers explained to David that the world had become a terrible place. He explained that the majority of mankind was wretched and didn't deserve to live. He had a plan to rid the world of the bad, ReSet, and start over, only using the good. He had ideas on how to maintain the good. He had selected nine other people in the United States that he felt had a strong moral code that could help re-establish this New World ReOrder. He wanted them to serve as chairmen beside him. Ten people who would collaborate and choose the best course of action and plans for how the world should move forward. He felt David King was one of those individuals. Moreover, he wanted him to be his right-hand man. He said he was impressed that after such a tragic loss, David hadn't given up but rather focused all his efforts and finances on helping. He didn't let David ask many questions but simply slipped his business card into

David's front shirt pocket and walked away, disappearing into the crowd. It hadn't taken David very long to decide that this strange man was correct. The world was corrupt and unfair, and somebody needed to do something. Countless groups had tried and failed. He realized it was because it was on too small of a scale. He knew a change needed to happen. He saw firsthand working in the medical field that innocent people were hurt because of others' decisions. He realized he had nothing left to lose, and after a year of trying to do something good with his life, this could be that opportunity. He didn't have all the details yet, but he knew that he wanted to be a part of whatever Grayson Jeffers was planning. Not only did he become a part of it. He did exactly what Jeffers wanted, he became chair number two.

UTOPIAN UNITED

Did you hear me, Dave? I said we're ready, said Alford Newsome. David shook his head and stared blankly at Al. He wasn't sure how long he had slipped into his mental escape and was a little embarrassed about it. "I just finished the last code. The behavior bar is in effect. We're ready to gather the citizens in the town square and get started. Can you grab the origin tree? I'm going to get Beth and the kids and meet you there," continued Al.

"How's Charlie doing with all this change?" asked David, fully back to reality.

"It's getting easier. He pretty much grew up at Alpha, so moving is hard. He's of the age of accountability, and he's had all the training, though, so I don't think his behavior will be a problem. He's a great help to his little sister. However, I do know it must be hard seeing her misbehaving when he himself isn't allowed to. This will be the first live behavior bar, so I think everyone will have a tough time getting used to it. In a lot of ways, it'll be like living in Alpha, but in a lot of ways, it'll be brand-new territory," replied Al.

David shook his head in agreement. He was secretly relieved that Grayson hadn't asked him to head up a key city. Four of the chairs had volunteered without any fight, in true ReSet fashion. Grayson didn't want them to be all family men, so he knew he may be selected. These ten chairmen had done so much together in the last couple years. Grayson had traveled the United States hand-selecting them. In a way, there was a sense of tremendous pride they felt in knowing that this man had thought so highly of them. Each was one of only nine people worthy enough to be kept alive and to start a New World ReOrder. The United States had truly gotten so bad. Typically, the moral compass of citizens balances the corruption of politicians, but that didn't seem to be the case anymore. No doubt, since the beginning of the world, bad had outweighed the good. It didn't seem that many people cared about anyone other than themselves. Families even turned against families. There had been a huge war in the surrounding countries and how the leadership of the land that Grayson had always fought to defend responded unveiled the true intentions of how far the American citizenry had fallen.

At the time, Grayson was a retired five-star Army general and was responsible for all the nuclear codes. He was top dog. The Army was all he knew and what he loved. He had never married, had children, or done any of the normal things that a man does. He ate and slept the Army and loved every minute of it, quickly moving up the ranks. He had a knack for war. It was almost haunting to hear people describe him in battle. They said it's as if his eyes hungered for war. He only had one near-death moment where his career could have ended. One of his men stepped on an IED—an improvised explosive device. He heard the five-second clicking and knew immediately what it was. He ran toward his soldier, screaming to the rest of his squad to fall back. As the device went off, he tackled his soldier and rolled him into the brush. The soldier was unscathed but General Jeffers was not. The IED was rigged with homemade shrapnel and pieces of it shot through his back and into his chest. He was on the operating table for over seven hours. It didn't seem likely he would recover after a blast like that. However, he beat the odds and did just that. The doctors were unable to remove all the shrapnel, though, and he still had two pieces lodged near his heart. He said it was his personal reminder that you must die to serve the good of another. It was a scar he said he was proud to wear.

There was a raging war in the Middle East that had created a huge chain reaction for the surrounding countries of the US, and some of her allies were being attacked. Because of his experience and reputation, General Jeffers was called into the Whitehouse by the president himself to help devise the best course of action. Grayson knew, without a doubt that the solution was to go and help the allies. He argued that we needed to hold up the agreement we had with them and help them fight. He was confident that they would see what he was saying and agree. After all, he was the expert, and he knew exactly how to handle the situation. He planned to offer his services and stay to develop a foolproof plan. The president and his cabinet listened to the entire presentation. Almost with no hesitation, the president said no. Grayson was baffled. He wasn't used to hearing no, especially when it came to war. The president said, from that point forward, the United States was no longer going to bail out other countries, friend or foe. Grayson argued that it was the right thing to do. He stated that there was an understanding—that their allies helped with imports and exports and the US provided defense. The president didn't want to listen anymore and demanded that he leave. Grayson was irate and began screaming at the president. With coldness in his eyes, the president stripped Grayson of his rank and demanded he be removed from the premises. Grayson felt as if he was having a heart attack. As he was dragged from the oval office, the devotion he once felt turned cold.

When the president bailed in this manner, he sealed the fate of the United States. The president immediately shut off all help, and the allies were furious. The president took it a step further and decided that it was time for the United States to be fully self-sufficient, and he shut down all business with any outside countries. This included shipments, partnerships, and all communications. The United States had become its own dark cloud on the world map. He sent out a world-wide message indicating this change to all the countries and warned that if any tried to rise against his decision, a nuclear warhead would be headed their way. The world was in shock as what was once the strongest of the strong had completely gone off grid. One country attempted to invade, angry that the US had neglected everyone. To everyone's surprise, however, the president wasn't bluffing. A nuclear warhead obliterated the small country and all that inhabited it. As Grayson watched things unfold on the news, he knew it was time to finally do something. He needed to set things right; it was clear that the current leadership was incompetent. That's when the changes started. The president started something he wasn't ready for. The United States hadn't done what it needed to prepare itself for full separation. No doubt, she was capable but not without preparation. Supplies ran scarce, and people's true colors started to show. Crime rates, poverty, and death were at an all-time high. Grayson knew it wouldn't be long before the people of the US would destroy themselves and everything he had ever fought for from the inside out. He knew he was the man who could fix it all. This jump-started his mission of finding the five hundred people left in the world who were still "good". He would take those people and set up a new world. Together, they would bring back hope for all humanity.

He knew this meant killing over three hundred million people. He also knew at the rate the US was going, they were doing that already. This was the only choice. He knew he would need a team behind him. There would be ten chairs that ran the New World ReOrder. He would be the head, he would choose a trustworthy second, and the remaining eight would be support. It took him a good bit of research and travel to find them, but he did it. He found the best men to serve alongside him to help restore and heal America. It took them another year to find the remaining people who would serve as citizens. They had to basically kidnap them and bring them back to Alpha, the head city that Grayson had built, then tell them what was going to happen. Most people refused to go along with it at first, but Grayson had a way of awakening their minds to the idea that this was the right way to go. In time, they also learned it was really their only option unless they fancied being a part of the millions set to be eradicated. Then, came the worst part. Grayson had separated the men into fractions and split them up all over the United States. Since he first started this plan, even before selecting his chairs, he had gone to smaller cities and secretly planted undetectable gas clouds, weapons of mass destruction he had built himself. The Army had locked away his blueprints in a secret database for potential future use, but to his knowledge, nothing had ever been created—well, except for the thousands he had made in his basement. It was scary what Grayson Jeffers' mind could concoct. He was definitely a man you wanted on your side.

The gas clouds were small canisters much like an IED that you placed in the ground. However, you only needed four of them. You put the coordinates of the city into each device, and then when you entered a code remotely, the canisters would communicate with each other and connect. They each sent a surge of toxic gas he had created called seroxide into the sky and created a cloud that fell on that unsuspecting city, killing the entire population—instantly. This was the quickest way to take care of the cities. Yet, certain places required more action. Guns, fires, and bombs were used in these cases. The entire process took another year to complete. News spread quickly of the mass genocides that were happening. There was no evidence pointing to the source, and it created mass paranoia for the majority of America. A lot of the killing was done for the chairs because citizens were turning on each other at an alarming rate, even more so than before Grayson began his mission. Some of the chairs didn't seem bothered; they said it was for the greater good, and they all believed it. Grayson had drilled it into their brain enough, and they all had a private cause, but Alford Newsome had the hardest time with it. He puked after almost every mission. He was almost unrecognizable when he came back that year.

David assumed that was the reason he had volunteered his family so quickly when Grayson was ready to start the ReFresh. He felt that Al wanted a chance to do something to balance what he had been involved in. Grayson had provided two years to let the world settle and then picked one city in each point of the US: North, South, East, and West. He needed a chair to head up that city and be the example. He said it would be on a volunteer basis, unless there weren't enough volunteers. This wasn't an issue, even though they knew they were taking a chance. If the new cities reached a level of "bad" like the world had done, Grayson Jeffers and the chairs would send a team in to ReSet that city. Although the chair member and their family would be spared, the death of that city would be their personal responsibility. Grayson was determined that if people now lived knowing their extinction was a possibility, they would straighten up. With the chairs volunteering, they were ready for the next phase. Chair #3, Alford Newsome, and his family would be heading West. His original city, Vicksburrow, was now Utopian. Chair #6, Bo Billings, would be heading North. His original city, Ravensburg, was now Phoenix. Chair #7, Slate Lloyd, would be headed South. His original city, Port Leah, was now Evermore. Finally, Chair #9, Seth Detlan, would be headed East, his original city, Castiloass, was now Morality.

David's cell phone vibrated. He looked down at it and recognized the number immediately. "Hey, G.J., how are things at Alpha?" He spent a few minutes on the phone reassuring Grayson that everything was going well. He wished he wasn't here for this. He was sent for two reasons today, and one of them he didn't feel right about. The first was obvious, and Al had no reason to second-guess his presence. Everyone back at Alpha wanted a live report of how the first new key city's grand opening was going. Sure, they had already implanted each citizen, so they were getting feedback. The five-second delay wouldn't cause an issue because they would still see and hear everything, but they wanted a report from somebody who wasn't a citizen. They wanted to see if all their work had paid off. The best way to do that was to send a chairman in to get all the information and report back. Grayson wasn't just calling for a friendly check-in; he wanted information.

The second reason he was there wasn't revealed to Al. Grayson had started wondering about Alford's allegiance. Even though he had been the biggest champion from the inception of this plan, a few recent visits back to Alpha had caused Grayson some concern. He had spoken to him personally, and Al had reassured him that everything was okay. He had said it was just the nerves of Utopian's opening day, but part of Grayson's success in life was due to his keen skill of reading people, and something just felt off about Al. He wanted David there to monitor all his moves on opening day to make sure that Alford Newsome was sticking to the plan.

David hadn't dared argue with Grayson, but internally, this was killing him. Alford and his family had become a second family to him. He had already lost his wife; he didn't want to chance jeopardizing another relationship that he had allowed himself to develop. Despite that sickening sense of betrayal, he knew where his ultimate allegiance had to lie, and that was with Grayson. He looked at his watch and realized it was time to start; he had to get to the town square.

As David pulled into the square, it became clear that the citizens of Utopian had already gathered. There were a hundred people of all ages, sexes, and ethnicities standing at full attention. They had erected a small platform in front of the square where the Newsome family was sitting. It was a very pretty city that Grayson had selected. Behind the square was a large pond, fully stocked, and behind them in the distance, gigantic identical lamp posts marking the city park entrance could be seen.

The Newsome family looked perfect sitting on that platform. He felt confident that Al was still on board, and no doubt his family was the perfect choice for this first city. He parked the truck, and Charlie immediately left the stage to help him.

"Hey, Uncle Dave! Got any advice for me today?" Charlie asked.

Dave's inner guilt deepened when he heard Charlie call him Uncle Dave, a nickname Charlie had given him when he was only two years old. David ruffled Charlie's hair and smiled at him.

"Just be yourself, Char. You're the finest kid I know."

Charlie's grin stretched from ear to ear, and this seemed to calm any nerves he'd previously had. He jumped into the back of the truck to help get the tree and then ran back to the podium to take his seat. He knew better than to be late. David carried the Origin tree, a baby weeping willow, behind the podium and began planting it in a pre-dug hole.

Alford Newsome stood up from his chair, looked at his wife, kissed the top of her head, and stood behind the pulpit and microphone that had been set up. "People of Utopian, this is a glorious day. I know these past few years have been difficult, to say the least. Take pride in the fact that, through it all, you have remained good. You have remained moral. You are the future. Look to your left and to your right. These people standing next to you are here for you. We all have the same goal: be good, stay good, and create good. I know you were all apprehensive about being implanted with the monitoring devices. Let me assure you, however: that is a necessary measure. I know it has already been explained, but as mayor of your town, I want to make sure you hear it from me as well. You will have your privacy. When you are using the bathroom or head to bed for the evening, just scan your hand outside of each of those corresponding rooms and your feed will be disabled. Let me remind you that for the bathroom, it is only for ten minutes at a time, so please don't forget to rescan your hand. If you don't, that's okay, as the system will automatically do it for you, but each time you forget, the behavior bar climbs. Also, at night, only scan when you are ready for sleep. Your bed monitors your vitals, so if you're not in your bed ready for sleep when you scan, that will also go against you. The whole point is to create a city that is good. We are being monitored by Alpha and the ReSetters to ensure that is exactly what we are doing. Every billboard in this town has been modified to show the Behavior Bar. When any citizen in this town does something "bad", it will ding, and a city alarm will sound. There is no action worse than the other, except physically harming another; that is an immediate ReSet.

Grayson wants us all to remember the entire goal of this city is to recreate a world that is once again good. We all need to work toward that. For example, taking something and lying hold the same weight. Each "bad" action equals a mark. Pay close attention to this bar. It's percentage-based, but we can get 5,000 marks every five years. We all know what happens if it reaches the very top. If you look behind me, Mr. King has finished planting our origin tree. Thank You, Mr. King. This willow will grow quickly. It will stand at approximately ten feet in five years. That will be seen from one side of the city to the next. When we make it to our five-year mark—and we will make it—we'll get our first ReFresh on our Behavior Bar. We'll also get our new permanent city sign to mark that special day. I know it's a lot to take in, but remember, this is for the greater good. Let's say the ReSetter motto together. Be good. Someone is always watching. Remember that is for everyone's protection. So, let's celebrate this very special day. Let us remember that we are all, including myself and my family, in this together. We are Utopian, united.

THE NEWSOME'S REVEALED

~ Chair #3

Around of applause erupted as the entire city of Utopian cheered on their new leader. Alford smiled warmly at them as he backed away from the pulpit to join his now-standing family. His wife slipped her arm around his waist and squeezed. She knew he hated public speaking and was trying to be supportive.

Katie giggled as she twirled around the stage, oblivious to the gravity of the situation. Her father told her to stop twirling, and she immediately obeyed. He sighed with relief. He knew he had put pressure on his family. Trying to be good was already a hard task, let alone being the family who was supposed to set the example. His family pretty much needed to be perfect. As if Beth was reading his mind, she leaned closer and whispered into his ear, "We can do this." He put his arm around her and squeezed her shoulder in response. He knew they could. He put his free arm around Charlie as someone requested a picture. They promised him it would be in the morning paper.

The crowds began dispersing throughout the town, taking in their surroundings and trying to adjust to what they would now be calling "home". Grayson and his chairs had been very selective in what families lived in which town. They even mapped out everyone's living arrangements. They had set up each city to give it the best shot so the citizens could live "good" lives. They had also given everyone new jobs. These towns were like towns in the US before the change. They had police and fire stations, post offices, veterinary clinics, department stores, markets, movie theaters, parks, schools, and restaurants. The two main things that were missing were a hospital and a courthouse. Grayson had trained everyone that minor medical situations would all be treated at the vet's office, which doubled as a clinic. Grayson had selected either a vet or a doctor for each town but not both. To him, medical stuff was much the same whether it was a human or an animal. Anything major or life-threatening was all done at Alpha, where they had a full clinic for treating patients. The closest key city to Alpha, Utopian, was six hours away, but Grayson had rounded up four airplanes, modified them, and stocked them with medical supplies turning them into his very own airborne ambulances for that very purpose. He had a team of medical doctors that stayed at Alpha that was on reserve in case such an incident occurred. From the five hundred people he had kept alive, four hundred were for the cities, but the remaining one hundred were Team Alpha. They lived with the remaining chairs and Grayson at Alpha and served different purposes. Most importantly, they were all trained on how to perform a town ReSet if it ever came to that. Grayson was confident that his plan was foolproof, and such an event would never come to pass.

"What do we do now, Father?" Katie asked.

"Now, you go home with your momma and get dinner ready, and I'll be home soon. I'm just going to walk around town making sure everything is going all right and that people are getting settled in. I think I'll go talk to the sheriff too and make sure everything is good on his end," her father replied.

"How long do you think you'll be?" Charlie asked.

"No more than a couple hours," Father answered.

Both kids smiled at their dad and shook their heads, careful not to argue.

Smiling, Beth leaned in and kissed her husband on the cheek. "You call me if you need anything at all."

"I will indeed," Alford replied to her.

With that, Beth took both of her children by the hand and headed down the brick roads of the town toward their house. It was a large breathtaking white house on the hill. You could see it from any angle in the town. It was directly across from the city park. Her front view porch was also beautiful. It overlooked the town square, the pond, and now the willow. The park, with its impressive lamp posts, completed the scene. She assumed Grayson had picked it as a reminder that the whole town was always watching. She had never really liked Grayson, but she believed in her husband, and he had convinced her that they were doing the right thing. He had convinced her that too many innocent people were made to suffer due to the choices of people who were evil, corrupt, and wicked.

She had never been pessimistic. Her parents had raised her to see the beauty in everyone, always forgive, and do kind things unto others, no matter how they treated you. She lived that life and lived it well. Even when her parents had died in a car crash after a drunk driver hit them, she found a way to cope. She started a volunteer hotline. If you were ever somewhere and in need of a designated driver, you could call Beth's hotline number and she would arrange you a ride, free of charge. Her program had grown so large that many of the surrounding cities had started them as well. With each ride that was given, contact information was shared, and she would follow up with the individuals to educate them more on the dangers of drinking and driving. Coincidentally, she met Alford there. He was one of her hotline volunteers. His sister had died from a drunk-driving incident, and he too wanted to do something to change the world for the better. He wasn't the typical handsome that turned girl's heads, but she was drawn to him in a way she had never experienced. It was easy for her to get a date, but she usually turned down any prospecting suitors. However, something about Alford Newsome intrigued her. The two started sharing stories at the end of one of her training sessions, and before they even realized it, everyone had left, and they were the last two there. Much to his surprise, he leaned over and tucked her hair behind her ear. It caught him off guard to do something so intimate to someone he had just met. It was odd for him because if felt so organic. The sparks were instant. They had begun dating that very night and started working together on the hotline program. They had seen so many people personally stop drinking and driving and some who were abusing alcohol give it up altogether. She knew she had found a way of turning something tragic into something not only good but beautiful. She was helping people, and she had found her soulmate. She had felt like it was the purest way to honor her parents. She cringed now, considering what her parents would say about her. Her views had changed on people. Her hope in humanity had changed. She was no longer naïve. She removed her hand from her daughter's hand and placed it on her stomach as a tear rolled down her cheek. It had been many years since she had thought about Avery.

***

It was a cold Christmas Eve as Alford dashed across the street with his wife's gloved hand in his. She laughed and giggled as the snow began falling harder. A large flake fell on her nose, and she twitched it, as the snow melted. He turned just at the right time to witness it and stopped and pulled her in close. She stopped laughing and looked at him as he gazed at her. She began to blush and asked him what he was doing.

"I love when you do that," he replied. He knew she hated her nose twitch and was embarrassed he had seen her do it. He didn't want to give her a chance to respond and ruin the moment, though, so he quickly kissed her nose and began running again.

"Are you ever going to tell me what we're doing?" she asked.

He looked over his shoulder, shook his head, and kept running. They ran another half block, and he stopped, with his wife bumping into him. He walked behind her, put his hands over her eyes, and told her to walk slowly and trust him. He had a surprise for her. She was very excited to see the surprise but more excited to tell him her news later. They had just celebrated their two-year anniversary and it was always the same. They went to the same restaurant they had on their first date, Gemi's, then always ended with cheesecake and coffee at their favorite bakery. Last year, Alford hadn't had a surprise for her, and she hadn't had one for him, so this made this anniversary extra special.

"We're here," he said, interrupting her thoughts.

He removed his hands from her eyes, and it took them a second to adjust. When they finally did, they were blurry again as the hot tears welled up in them.

"Oh, I love it," she replied. She turned and buried her head in Alford's chest. She couldn't believe he had done this.

She was staring at the cutest little building next to a park that said Mamaw and Papaw's Helpline. Alford had purchased a storefront for their helpline service. It was a baby blue building with black shutters and a black and white striped French canopy hanging over the door. There was one small window in the front with a flower box full of daisies in it. Mamaw and Papaw was what her parents had requested to be called as grandparents but sadly never got that chance. Alford had chosen this name to share their love with the many people they helped. He had said it was giving them—that chance to be grandparents to a ton of people. Beth had said for years she wished they had a storefront so they could do more and help more people. Operating from their living room had become almost counterproductive. She still couldn't believe she finally had a shop.

Alford pulled a pair of keys from his pocket and waved them in front of her. "You wanna go in?"

She smiled and checked her watch. It was almost 9 and they had to hurry. "I do, but after cheesecake and coffee, I have a surprise of mine own."

Alford looked dumbfounded. "Well, Mrs. Newsome, I am genuinely intrigued," he said.

She hugged him tightly and thanked him for being so wonderful. Then, she grabbed his hand, ready to be the leader this time. As they ran back the way they had come and turned the corner, Beth hit something hard, and it knocked her down. Alford was shocked and bent over to help his wife when he felt the most incredible pain in his head, and it knocked him down. He groaned as he heard his wife scream. He rolled over to his side and saw three men grabbing her purse. He shakily stood to his feet, his head pounding, and he felt a trickle of blood running down the side of his face.

"Beth, just give it to them," he said. "Don't fight. Here, take my wallet and my watch, too."

He knew it was best to just comply. He wasn't worried about the money. He just wanted the men to leave; he just wanted to keep his wife safe. He could hear his wife sobbing as he stumbled toward her. The men didn't hesitate to take his possessions too and then began to walk off. He made it to Beth and knelt to check on her.

"It's okay. It's all over now," he said. He didn't even notice that they had come back.

"On second thought," one of the men growled, "that's not all we want."

"What else do you want? Please, we don't want any more trouble," Alford begged.

"Trouble is who we are," the same man replied.

Two of the men grabbed Alford and pulled him back and held him by the arms as the other man circled around Beth, who was whimpering on the ground with her arms around her knees.

"Don't you touch her," Alford yelled, desperately trying to break free from their grasp. The largest man, who seemed to be in charge, pulled out a gun, which made a sickening click-click. This got both of the Newsomes' attention.

"Be still, or your lady here will eat lead," the man said coldly. Beth whimpered more.

"Beth, I love you," Alford said.

She continued to cry as Alford continued to try and break free despite the man's threats. For the next few minutes, Alford watched as that man beat his wife. He repeatedly kicked her in the ribs, stomach, and face. The three men laughed and joked as if they were at a ball game. Alford screamed repeatedly for him to stop, but he couldn't overpower his captors. He had to endure every sickening second. Finally, his wife looked over at him, one eye completely swollen shut, and then she closed her eyes and her breathing slowed. He nodded to the two men and Alford again felt a painful blow to the back of his head. He fell to the ground, and everything began to go black. He crawled to where his wife lay and tried to yell for help. The blood was filling his eyes, and his head was spinning. He was unable to keep moving and reached out to just touch her as he passed out.

***

The next time they saw each other was at the hospital. Somebody had walked by, saw them both on the ground, and called 911. Beth had internal injuries and had to undergo surgery immediately. Her face was swollen, and she was almost unrecognizable. Alford had suffered a concussion and needed stitches in two different places in his head. As they wheeled his hospital bed into his wife's room, he didn't want to face her. He had failed her. He was supposed to keep her safe and he had done nothing. He hated himself for it. When he finally made it beside her, she didn't even move. He didn't know what to say, so they just sat in silence for the longest time looking at each other, looking at the damage that those men had caused. Finally, he slipped his hand between the bars of their hospital beds and grabbed hers. He squeezed it, and after a few moments, she squeezed back. He managed to mouth the words I'm sorry to her before he began to sob. She squeezed his hand, and he stopped and tucked her hair back as he had done that very first night. She cringed at first to his touch. Not because it was him but rather because of what had happened.

"We're going to get through this, and we're going to find the men that did this," Alford said.

She stared at him blankly. She was reviewing their whole life in her head. They had done so much good for so many people who didn't deserve it, how could this have happened? She didn't feel very optimistic right now. She didn't feel like forgiveness. She didn't recognize herself. "I don't think I'll be able to be me after this," she said weakly. "They took everything, Al."

"No, honey, they didn't. We're alive. We'll make more money. We'll go have that cheesecake. We'll run Mamaw and Papaw's Hotline. We'll find the good in this; you'll see," he said.

"Not this time," she replied.

He was so confused. His Beth had never acted like this. She had overcome so much; he knew that, with time, she would do the same with this. "You just need time, honey. It will get better with time," he said as he kissed her hand.

She pulled her hand back, which caught him off guard. "I was pregnant," she said.

His eyes widened and he felt the color drain from his face. He opened his mouth to speak, but no words came out.

"I was pregnant. They took everything because I lost the baby. I was going to tell you over cheesecake and coffee. That was my surprise. We lost her; we lost our baby ..." She cried and turned her head.

"Her?" he asked. "We were having a girl."

Beth turned her head again, and her eyes filled with tears. "Yes. I was four months pregnant, and now the doctors don't even know if I will have kids because of the damage."

Alford began crying. They wanted a family full of kids and he couldn't believe what she was saying. How had he not realized she was pregnant? He felt a darkness inside his heart—directed toward those men and, strangely, toward the world. He looked back at his wife and didn't know what to say to her. He loved her so much, but he didn't know how they would get through this.

"A girl?" he asked again in disbelief.

Beth shook her head as more tears fell from her eyes. "Avery." She replied.

TEACH THEM YOUNG

Mama, aren't you going to come in? Charlie asked.

His momma had been standing outside the house looking off in the distance for the last several minutes, and he was starting to get worried. He had already taken his sister in and gotten her a snack. He had come back, and she was still standing in the same spot on the front porch, hugging the navy and white striped swing pillow with the family's handprints on it that they had made her for Mother's Day. He had tried to speak to her once already, but he was sure the Alpha watch team was already doing its job, and he didn't want to seem disrespectful. There was no way that he was going to be the reason that the town got its first mark. He knew it would probably happen eventually, but not on opening day, and certainly not by him.

He had been training for this for the last three years, and he was determined to make his parents—especially his father—proud. This was the first live key city since the world had been obliterated, and they needed it to be successful. He knew the remaining three cities would only be started once they saw how Utopian would do. Their city would serve as the guinea pig. He had overheard his father asking Mr. Grayson Jeffers for a week to adjust, but there was no budging from Mr. Jeffers. He was a harsh man, and Charlie had mixed emotions about him. On one hand, he felt a strange yearning to be close to him because the only life he really remembered was his time at Alpha since his family was moved there when he was two years old, but on the other hand, he felt very uncomfortable when he was near him. He saw him every day, but he was the only person at Alpha that Charlie hadn't really spent much quality time with. At age five, he was so excited to finally start kindergarten. His momma read him a bedtime story every night, and he was in love with all of them. They were full of far-away places, valiant heroes, and remarkable characters. He didn't like the mushy stuff much, but his momma did, and he loved her; so, he endured. Every story was like a training manual for a life he knew nothing about. Alpha was so isolated, and they were never allowed to leave the building. They didn't get to experience a fraction of what the characters in his momma's stories got to. There was an interior courtyard, with massive sunroofs and a large playground where the kids got to burn off their daily pent-up energy. Sometimes, he just sat at the top of the slide and looked up to the sky—right at the sun. He longed to feel its actual warmth. Grayson acted as if he had done the children a favor by adding this element, but for Charlie, it was a sad reminder of things he would never have. His parents had cautioned him to be grateful that he was one of the children allowed to survive. This often confused him and played with his emotions. It made him feel guilty for ever feeling envious and upset about his home at Alpha. So, he tried to suppress those feelings and just longed for the evening stories his momma read. Every time his momma read a story, he would close his eyes and put himself inside it. He never told his momma, but he wanted a grand adventure like the characters in those stories had.

When it was time for school and his momma told him he would learn to read for himself, he was elated. He did learn, but what he wasn't prepared for was the fact that his first year of school would also double as his first year of training for the New World ReOrder. Every kindergarten had now reached the age of accountability, which initiated their training. They were taught about what ended the world in the first place. The information was overwhelming.

They were too young to hear about death, especially of such an extreme nature and on such a massive scale. He remembered crying as he was forced to look at some of the photos after the desolation. He had a very hard time coming to grips with the fact that his Uncle Dave and specifically his father would have a part in everything that had happened. It took him months to process everything; he was only five and it was just too much. Eventually, he and the rest of the children became numb to what they were being told and started accepting it. They weren't given a choice but to accept it, but even if they had a choice, something now told Charlie he would still accept it. Grayson Jeffers had a haunting way of speaking to people. It was as if he took over your soul and synced it with his, so you, too, saw things the way he saw things despite your personal feelings about it.

By the end of his kindergarten year, he walked across a stage after a cheesy performance with his class. He was handed a rolled-up paper certificate that had shown his achievements. Immediately after the ceremony, his entire class was also ushered to another ceremony. This one was to celebrate their achievement of completing their Alpha program. They were now fully accountable for anything bad that they did. They were also fully aware that because of their bad actions, their entire city could be killed just like Grayson's team of ReSetters had done before. It was a lot of pressure on the children, but Grayson didn't care. This ceremony was special. Instead of a paper certificate, the Alpha doctors inserted their monitoring devices into each child. Each person who would be relocated to a new key city was to be implanted with these monitoring chips. The adults already had them, and the children only got them after their accountability training. Grayson, always planning for the worst-case scenario, was paranoid and wanted to ensure there was no way that any of the citizens would "wise up" and try to remove chips, so each one was implanted in a random location. Since it didn't matter where they were placed because of how they worked, he knew this was the best way to ensure nobody went looking for their chip. Each chip contained nanobots that exited the chip and entered the bloodstream of the "host." The chip then sent a signal that kept the nanobots active. The signal was powered by the body's natural electric charge. As long as you were breathing, the signal was active. The bots were then able to tap into the central nervous system, which gave the team at Alpha full access to each person's auditory and optic nerves, allowing Grayson Jeffers and his team of observers to see and hear everything as if they were doing it themselves. This was how Grayson Jeffers intended to monitor how "good" the city was being. He had truly thought of everything ... except how to eliminate the five-second delay. Once something was said or done, it took five seconds to relay through the chip's signal and send the feed to the observers monitoring stations. He didn't feel like five seconds particularly mattered, though. As long as he could catch anyone who was being bad, the system would work just fine. Once the action was complete, it wasn't as if the person could take it back. The team would catch it, send the warning bell out, and raise the behavior bar. He didn't really think they would need to do it that much because he felt he had done a great job of explaining to everyone exactly why they were where they were in the world and what needed to be changed for the good of the future. These citizens would be foolish to act immorally. He had observed them all at Alpha, and there were very few incidents, so he was confident, as always, that he had chosen the perfect 500 people. He knew people, and he had no doubt he had just created the perfect New World.

Realizing he, too, had drifted into his own thoughts, Charlie came back to the present and saw his mother was still in her own headspace. He had seen her do that only once before, and it had scared him then too. She wouldn't tell him then what she was thinking about, and he didn't expect her to do so now either.

He slowly walked over to her and placed his hand on her arm and just left it there. His mother had taught both of her children that if they needed to speak to her and she was talking to someone else, especially an adult, it was best to just rest their hand on her arm. She would realize that they needed her, and she would find an appropriate time in the conversation to stop and acknowledge them. She had also taught them that if it was truly an emergency, they could tap their index finger three times and she would acknowledge them sooner. She had started teaching courses at Alpha a year ago to mothers and children on ways to "be polite". She had requested to do so because she felt it would be necessary before moving into the city. Grayson had said no at first. Charlie remembered how upset she was that he had denied it. One week later, she came home with a grin on her face and kissed Father on the head. He had commented about how chipper she seemed, and he vividly remembered her saying how she had won with Grayson Jeffers. She had also commented that he wasn't untouchable, and everyone had a weak spot; you just had to find it. The look in her eyes was unlike any he had ever seen, and it was a bit alarming. His mother's eyes were always soft and kind, but this was mischievous.

His hand had rested on her arm for about thirty seconds, and she still wasn't responding. He felt as if it was becoming a bit of an emergency and he tapped three times. As if her maternal instincts kicked in, she immediately dropped the pillow she was holding, dropped to her knee, held his face in her hands, and stared at him. His eyes must have betrayed his alarm.

"Oh, Charlie, sweetie, I'm so sorry. Mommy was just thinking about something ... something, difficult. What's wrong?"

Charlie swallowed hard. He hadn't meant to upset his mom; he was just worried about her. He felt the moisture in his eyes begin.

"Oh, sweetie, don't cry," she said as she wiped his eyes with the corner of her sleeve.

"Will we get a mark for this, Mom?" he asked.

"Of course not dear," she replied. "Not for this. You're allowed to be upset. You're allowed to have emotions. We aren't meant to be robots. We're just meant to do good. Now, you tell me what is going on."

He knew better than to disobey. "Yes ma'am. I had said your name a long time ago and you weren't answering, so I was getting really worried that there was something wrong with you. I took Katie in and gave her a snack. I don't actually know how long it has been, but I was just worried, that's all."

She hugged Charlie tightly, and he welcomed it. His mother always smelled of flowers and honey. He remembered she had read a book once before about a bee who got lost after falling asleep on a semi-truck. This bee had wound up in another state before he finally woke. He was terrified and immediately panicked. He knew his mother bee would be fervently searching for him and the idea that he would be the reason she was worried made the experience that much worse. The little bee didn't know what to do and flew to a fence post to cry. After just a few moments he had caught the whiff of a very familiar smell in the air. It was the smell of a distinct and rare flower that he knew only grew on the farm where his bee family lived. He finally had an idea. He would follow his nose back to his family. He gave himself a quick pep talk to gain the courage to journey back not knowing how long it would take or what he would face. The bee did face some challenges, but as he got closer and closer, his courage increased. He just kept focusing on his family to motivate him to continue his mission. He got within one city of his family, and that exotic flower was now filling his nose to the point he could scarcely smell anything else. When he was on his final stretch home, he smelt his momma's famous beeberry cake, and his little bee wings flapped faster than ever. His mother had made this cake for him, for his birthday. He finally made it to their home of flowers his father had built and saw his momma holding that cake in one of the windows with tears in her eyes. He had done it! He had made it home. His mother had then explained that when she called the kids in for dinner, and he hadn't come she didn't know what to do or where to look. What she did know was that he was alive; she felt it in her antennas. He had been gone for four days, but she said at each meal, she made a fresh beeberry cake in hopes that wherever he was that maybe, just maybe, he would smell it and come home. The entire bee family reunited and enjoyed that most special cake that evening.

Charlie had always loved that story and when he learned to read, it was the first story he read back to his momma. Every time he hugged his momma, he thought of that story, and it made him smile.

"Well, Son, I'm terribly sorry for the scare, but I'm okay. Everything is okay. You'll see. Things are going to be just fine for us and for our family. This is our new start, and it's going to be great. Now, let's get inside and get dinner ready. I expect your father is done checking in and will be home shortly with lots of stories to tell," Momma said.

Charlie nodded his head in agreement, helped her stand up, and slipped his arm around her waist. He loved his momma so much. He was so excited to hear about everything that his father had seen in the town. He had secretly wanted to be right by his side, but he'd been too afraid to ask. He was close to his parents, but he knew there would be a slight adjustment since there was now continuous monitoring of their every move.

"You think everything is as it should be down there?" he asked.

"Dear, it's only been a few hours. I'm sure everything is going according to plan," she replied with a smile.

As if fate was listening to their private conversation and had another idea, a warning bell rang throughout the city. Charlie turned to see his mother frozen, fear filling her eyes. Someone had already made a mistake.

STRIKE ONE

Charlie kept staring at his momma, hoping what he thought had happened hadn't actually happened. His sister running out of the house crying confirmed the worst. Katie threw herself into her mother's arms and began whimpering. She wasn't at the age of accountability yet, but her parents had done a fine job teaching her early. She knew she still needed to be good even though her bad behavior wouldn't change the city's outcome yet. She had another year before that. That hadn't stopped their parents from encouraging her to start now. She was spared many of the gruesome details of death and destruction, but she understood the key points. She also understood when that solitary city bell rang, it meant that somebody in the city had done something bad. Mrs. Newsome pulled Katie back from her chest and wiped her face. She tried to give a reassuring smile, but Charlie saw right through it. She took a step forward to where Charlie was now standing, and she put her free arm around him as she was already doing for Katie. In unison, the three of them looked toward the closest billboard and watched the behavior bar change. A thin red line was now present where there had previously just been a void. Charlie was still dumbfounded as to who or what would have already caused this to happen. Everybody had known about the killings. Everyone had known how serious this was and how important this first key city was. Charlie looked back at his mother. She nodded her head in full understanding as if she was reading his mind; she had a knack for that.

"I'll keep supper warm for you both. Try to hurry back. Whatever your father needs, Son ..." she said.

"I'm there for him," he replied.

She smiled warmly, looked back at the behavior bar, sighed deeply, and took Katie by the hand, leading her back inside the house. Charlie watched for a minute as he followed his mother's silhouette to the kitchen counter. She had her hands resting on the counter and her head slumped down. Except for her outline, he couldn't see through the curtains, but he saw enough to know she was crying, and it hurt his heart. He turned away from their home and took off, sprinting, to find his father.

Alford Newsome was standing near the post office when it happened. He thought it was a sick joke at first. How in the world had someone already done something "*bad*"? He recited the words of his speech over again in his head. Had he confused the town? Had he not done a good enough job expressing the seriousness of this mission? He knew that it didn't matter how many years they had prepared; if this ended badly, Jeffers would blame him.

He headed on foot toward the sheriff's station to meet with the sheriff. He would have to launch a full investigation to figure out what had happened. After that, he assumed a town meeting would need to take place. He expected the town to be in full panic mode. He was right. As he walked down the street, families and citizens were standing outside their homes frozen in place staring at the behavior bar on the billboard. Some women were crying, and men were shaking their heads. They were all looking around, no doubt trying to find the culprit. Alford knew he needed to find them first, or this would turn into a witch hunt. He sped up his pace a bit and waved to people along the way. As he passed each one, he also muttered several pleasantries and reassuring remarks in an attempt to put everyone at ease. He knew it would only pacify the town for a short while before he would need to be more diplomatic. He passed the town square, and some families were already discussing the possibilities of what had happened and who they thought it was. Alford himself was starting to panic internally. He had to get a handle on this and wasn't currently making any progress. He had nearly convinced himself to break into a full sprint even though he was wearing his best suit and dress shoes. Luckily, as if being summoned, David came bumping along in his beat-up truck. Alford recognized the sputtering of the exhaust and didn't stop his forward progression toward the sheriff's station. David slowed his driving and opened the passenger door, never coming to a complete stop.

"What in the world, Al? Are you heading to the sheriff?" asked David.

"Yup," Alford simply replied, continuing to jog.

"You think you want to get in the car then and we can go together?" David asked.

Alford stopped jogging. Of course, this is what he needed to do. He needed a minute to think more clearly, or he wouldn't be able to make the decisions he needed to. A familiar voice flooded his thoughts.

"Father, what happened?"

He turned to see Charlie coming right at him in a blaze. Alford couldn't remember ever seeing him run that fast. His legs were a blur. Charlie barreled right into his father and hugged him tightly. Under any other circumstance, his father would have been elated. He squeezed him momentarily and gently pushed his son back by the shoulders. "Son, your mother does know you are here, correct?" his father asked while looking around cautiously.

"Yes sir, I had permission," Charlie replied.

Charlie saw relief spread across his father's face and he immediately read between the lines. "Oh, no, sir, I didn't cause this," he explained. "I asked to come find you after it happened."

His father wiped a bead of sweat from his forehead, thankful that he could find some solace in the fact his own boy hadn't set off the first alarm.

"You fellas getting in this truck or what?" David interrupted. "The town isn't looking very happy."

Immediately, both Charlie and his father jumped into the truck, and the three men headed toward the sheriff's station. The town wasn't very large, and they were parked out front within five minutes. As they pulled up, prepared to do massive detective work, they quickly realized this mystery wasn't going to take as long to solve as they had originally expected.

"Ah, there you are Mr. Newsome. Good news: I know what happened. Bad news: I'm what happened," the sheriff said as he turned around with his arm wrapped in what appeared to be a sheet. There was a bright red spot that had begun pooling in the middle of the sheet.

"Sheriff Tate, what happened to your arm?" asked Mr. Newsome. "What do you mean, you're what happened?"

"I'll explain, but I think you may need to get me to the town Vet-a-Doc because I'm feeling a little light-headed," he said as he fainted.

Mr. Newsome and David quickly reacted and loaded up the sheriff into the back of David's truck. As they were about to pull off, Alford noticed the door to the sheriff's station was shattered. He needed to get the sheriff some medical attention very quickly—and get some answers. The Vet's clinic was on the next street over. Dr. Nathaniel Allen was hesitant when Grayson told him that he would serve as both the vet and the town doctor for Utopian, but he knew there was no sense in arguing with him. He had made the comment that if he had wanted to work on people, that's what he would have gone to school for. Alford distinctively remembered Grayson slapping Dr. Allen on the back, chuckling, and saying that his schooling wouldn't matter at all if Grayson hadn't decided to spare him and his young wife, to begin with. This was Grayson's way of intimidating people. He knew that they would have no choice but to follow his plan—for the greater good.

David stopped the truck, and the men unloaded Sheriff Tate from the truck bed. Charlie ran ahead and opened the door for them. He hadn't been able to make sense yet of what was going on, and he was still frightened. His father had told him to ride in the back of the truck with the sheriff in case he regained consciousness. The blood that was on the sheet had covered more surface area, and Charlie had taken off his dress shirt to apply more pressure. He looked down, and his hands were still red with the Sheriff's blood. It made him queasy, but he knew he needed to be strong for his father. David and his father had just sat the sheriff down in one of the waiting room chairs and leaned his body against the wall. Of course, he didn't seem to mind because he was still unconscious.

"Dr. Allen," his father yelled as he entered the back area of the clinic, disappearing from Charlie's view.

"Charlie, come sit with the sheriff again and make sure he doesn't fall over," David said.

Charlie nodded his head obediently. He had been trained that all adults were authorities and demanded direct obedience. He didn't particularly want to sit next to the bleeding sheriff because he was afraid he would pass out himself, but he still knew that he needed to obey. This city didn't need another warning bell. He wondered how Team Alpha was reacting to this situation. More specifically, he worried about how Grayson Jeffers was reacting to the situation. Charlie heard a ringing from David's pocket. Although it was muffled, Charlie recognized it. Grayson had made it mandatory that each chair head use the same ringtone when he was calling so they never missed a call from him. David sucked the bottom of his lip and hesitated to grab the phone at first. Charlie had learned that David did this when he was extremely nervous or frightened. Charlie looked up to David; he and his sister even called him Uncle Dave. He knew that David always put on a good front for him whenever he was dealing with Alpha business. He did a great job, but he was unaware that Charlie had picked up on his nervous habit. He finally fished the phone out of his pocket and answered.

"Sir, we haven't talked to him yet. I know you saw everything, but we're still getting to the bottom of it. No, sir. I know we need to handle it, but he's currently passed out as I'm sure you're aware. No, sir. I'm not trying to make excuses, but I know that Al will be able..." His voice trailed off as he exited the clinic.

Charlie badly wanted to follow him out of the clinic and continue listening to the one-sided conversation, but he knew better. He had no way of proving it, but he was positive that in addition to Grayson implanting the monitoring chips into the people, he had probably also retrofitted each business with cameras and monitoring equipment. He glanced around the room quickly checking each corner of the pale blue walls. On one wall there was a mural of rainbow-colored paw prints and a dog and cat sharing an ice cream bone sundae. The image made Charlie smile. There were no cameras visible, but he wasn't surprised by that. Suddenly, feeling as if they were probably watching him in the clinic, he dropped his head and began swinging his feet in his chair. Even though he was only eight, he felt at times that he was an adult. He had been exposed to so much and had to help with so much. This is why his momma's bedtime stories were so important. He needed that escape. The sheriff began to moan, and Charlie was unsure what to do. The sheriff tried to stand, and Charlie knew that wasn't an option.

"Sheriff Tate, you've been hurt. Please sit back down," Charlie said. "Father, he's awake! Please hurry!"

"Stupid old buzzard," the sheriff said, still only semi-conscious.

Charlie hadn't seen any buzzards in the city. Not even when they were making their canvassing and building trips to establish the city. He figured the sheriff was dreaming. Thankfully, Charlie's father and Dr. Allen showed up.

"How do you not know what happened yet, Mr. Newsome?" Dr. Allen asked.

"The sheriff passed out before he could tell us, but the front door to the station is shattered," Al replied.

"Father, not to interrupt, but there seems to be a crowd gathering outside, and they don't seem so happy. Uncle Dave also got a call from Mr. Jeffers, and I'm not sure where he is," Charlie said.

"It's fine, Son. Don't worry. Everything will be fine. Please help Dr. Allen with whatever he needs, and I'll go speak to our town," his dad answered.

Charlie didn't like this plan. He didn't want to see what was underneath that sheet causing the now crimson stains. There were lots he didn't want to do, but disobedience was not an option. Not now, and not ever. He shook his head and stood up slowly. Dr. Allen had already propped the sheriff up and was helping him toward the back.

"Charlie, if you could just grab his hat and come on back, you can be my special assistant," the Dr. said.

Charlie forced a smile in reply. "Whatever you need sir, I'm happy to help."

Mr. Newsome began to exit as David came from around the back of the clinic. Al knew that whatever he was doing, he had bad news.

"What did he say, Dave?" Alford asked.

"He knows what happened, and he's furious. He said it was silly nonsense and needs to be handled," David replied.

"Well, what happened?" Al asked.

"About that ... yeah. He won't tell me," David replied.

Alford was dumbfounded. He was about to address the town for a mysterious "bad", and the one person who should have helped was leaving him high and dry. His face twisted in confusion.

Reading his expressions David answered his thoughts. "He wants to see how you rally and how you fix this. He said you've been training for this and he expects nothing short of an expedient and positive outcome."

Alford was still flustered by Grayson's decision, but he knew better than to let that resonate on his face. No doubt David's chip was activated, and Grayson was personally watching every move to see what Alford did. He had signed his family up for this; he knew the risks. He just hadn't expected to have to handle something this soon. This is why he had pushed so hard for that week of grace; everyone needed time to adjust, including himself.

He didn't have much time to prepare for a solution because more Utopianites were beginning to fill the streets and make their way to the clinic. He jumped into the back of David's rusted blue truck, climbed onto the roof, and began to address the town. He explained to everyone that the situation was identified and under control. He requested that everyone show up at the town square in one hour so he could give everybody a full explanation of what happened. He told them that he wanted everyone in attendance so he only had to explain it once. This appeased the town, and the crowd that had gathered scurried off. He knew that they probably weren't happy with the information, but he also knew that they wouldn't dare voice any objection since they were being watched and had already received their first strike. If nothing else, this proved to the town that Grayson Jeffer's plan was exactly as he said. Cities would be responsible for any bad that they did.

Alford jumped down from the truck and hurried back inside the vet's clinic. He only had one hour to figure out what in the world had happened and how he would fix it.

SILLY SHERIFF

Charlie had finished helping Dr. Allen and was back in the waiting room where David stayed with him. The men still had no idea what had happened, and they didn't want Charlie exposed to something he had no business hearing. David had offered to take Charlie home. Alford thought it was a good idea, but he could tell by the look in his boy's eyes that he wanted to be there for him. Alford had always admired how his son looked up to him. He knew that the only reason that Charlie had run all the way to town was to make sure his father was okay. He knew his son was young, but he had seen how mature he had grown throughout this process. They had gotten pregnant with Charlie only a year after their miscarriage, and he believed it was exactly what they needed. Their relationship had naturally gotten rocky, and although he loved Beth more than he thought he could ever love another person, the incident had put a brick wall in between them. Neither one of them seemed as if they were willing to pick up the sledgehammer to tear it down either. It was too painful to talk about that awful night. They didn't want to acknowledge that it had happened, let alone relive it each time they discussed it.

At different times, each of them had suggested a marriage counselor, but they never seemed to make the time. One night changed the course of their life once again, and when Beth found out she was pregnant, that wall slowly started crumbling, brick by brick. Decorating nurseries, buying baby clothes, and deciding on a name reunited the Newsome couple in a way that no marriage counselor could. They were terrified in the beginning, so afraid they would lose their unborn child. But on that cold October evening, when they delivered that tiny infant and held him in their arms, what had happened a year before packaged itself neatly in a small box and stored itself in the back of both of their minds. They didn't address it, but they stopped letting it consume their daily thoughts.

Indeed, Charlie had been what their marriage needed. The first eighteen months that they were new parents was Heaven on earth. They were the three amigos. Charlie was full of energy and a ray of light for both of his parents. It seemed as if each day, the love that he had for both his mother and father was enough for the whole family. Without him even knowing it, this tiny baby was keeping the love between his parents alive. It was infectious how loving their son was.

When he was a year old, almost to the day, he took his first steps. He was sitting on the floor playing with his blocks, and his mother had sneezed. This startled him and he turned just as his father had said "Bless you". She thanked him and went back to reading her book, while his father worked on the computer. Charlie had used the mahogany-stained coffee table that his father had built to help him stand many times so when he did this, his parents were not surprised. However, what happened next was something they were completely unprepared for. He moved around the side of the table, his hands trailing the wood-burned horse mural, let go, gained his balance, and then wobbled toward his parents without help. His mother dropped her book on the floor as his father shut his laptop and placed it on the couch. Then, he picked Charlie up and spun him around, the pride beaming from his face. His mother met him in his father's arms with applause and kisses.

Charlie loved the attention. In that moment, he grabbed both of their heads with his tiny arms, pulled them in close, and squeezed.

For the first time in a long time, Beth and Alford Newsome locked eyes and just stared. This sweet family had just shared a very special moment. As they looked at each other, it was noticeable that the pain that was once there didn't seem to be as strong. The joy and love that had always been there started finding its way back. Beth smiled slowly, and Alford cupped her face with his hand. This was something he had done when they were dating, and it gave her butterflies. She couldn't remember the last time he had done it. She closed her eyes and nuzzled his hand. This delighted Charlie, and he squeezed tighter. As if in each other's minds like they used to be, each parent kissed him on the cheek at the same time, which sent Charlie into full-belly laughter. In that moment, all was well again.

Now all these years later, Alford was terrified that in his quest to find justice for all the "Averys" of the world, he had robbed his son of a normal and happy childhood. The other option would have been death, but somedays, even though Alford believed in the cause, he found himself wondering which fate was worse. He thanked David for the offer but said it would be fine for Charlie to stay a little while longer. He could see the gratitude on Charlie's face. He patted him on the back and headed toward the back of the clinic alone. He paused outside the smoked-glass door with his hand on the handle for a moment. He stared at the vinyl lettering that read, "Dogs and Cats allowed – Fleas wait outside." He had come up with that saying himself when he and Dr. Allen were remodeling the clinic. Alford thought it was imperative to do as much to this city as he could to make everyone feel comfortable, despite the unorthodox situation they had found themselves in. He had always found laughter a comfort in his own home, and he wanted his town to be built around love and laughter. Each door had a unique saying like this. He had felt so prepared to take on this challenge. Now, he doubted he would last a week. He didn't want to be responsible for any more death. He had believed in this cause so strongly after Avery's death, and he'd wanted to see it through. However, an incident on day one was not what he'd signed up for. Taking a deep breath, he finally worked the nerve to push the door open. The whooshing sound of the door jolted Dr. Allen who had his back facing the door.

"Good thing I just finished up, or that could have gotten really dicey," Dr. Allen said. He stepped to the side to show what he was referencing. Sheriff Tate was lying on an operating table that was painfully clear was not made for humans. Sheriff Tate was not a small man, and almost every one of his appendages was hanging off the table. He groaned a little, Alford assumed from the pain.

He noticed his arm was covered in iodine and there was a row of stitches atop his forearm.

"Is he okay, Dr. Allen?" Al asked. "Can you tell what happened?"

"Not completely," he replied. "I can tell you glass was involved because I had to pull shards out of the wound on his arm. It was pretty deep in some places, which accounted for the blood loss, which probably also accounted for him passing out."

"Will he be okay?" Alford asked.

"Sure will," Dr. Allen replied. "Thanks to me, he won't have much of a scar either. I'm kinda a suture hero," he said with a chuckle. When he noticed Alford wasn't laughing, though, he stopped. "Hey, that was supposed to be a joke. Aren't you the guy who loves the funny stuff?" he asked.

Alford forced a smile. He was that guy. He had just tried to remind himself of that moments before. Typically, he would have found Dr. Allen's joke quite amusing. He and his son loved cheesy jokes like that. They called them their "dad jokes". He didn't want to seem rude to Dr. Allen.

"Yes, that's right. Sorry, it was quite clever." Alford said. "My brain is just so fixated on trying to figure out what happened, that I wasn't firing on all cylinders. My bad."

"Ah, I understand," Dr. Allen replied. "No worries. I'm just going to head out and clean up and let you two get down to business. I gave him a mild sedative to help keep him calm, but it should be wearing off any minute now."

"I appreciate it, doc," Alford replied. "We have that town meeting in about fifty-five minutes. Can I count on you to be there? It would be good for the town to hear exactly what you did."

Dr. Allen shook his head and smiled. "You betcha. See ya there," he said as he exited the room.

Alford grabbed a chair and rolled it beside the table. He wasn't exactly sure how long the medicine would take to wear off, but he was hoping it wouldn't be too much longer. He needed to do something with his time, so he began cleaning up the exam room. There were several medical supplies that the doctor had required to take care of the sheriff that had been left lying around. He was happy for the distraction. He put two surgical gloves on his hands and got to work.

It didn't take him but five minutes to clean the room, and he was back in his seat. He studied the stitches that were in the sheriff's arm and counted ten external sutures. He traced his finger along the smooth edges of the fresh wound. Dr. Allen wasn't wrong; he was excellent at sutures. When Alford was a kid, he had fallen into a barbed-wired fence. His mother had told him hundreds of times not to ride his bike so close to the fence line, but he was a boy, and he knew best. It hadn't helped that a couple of the neighborhood kids had dared him he couldn't ride with no hands near the fence for thirty seconds straight. He wasn't one to back down from a challenge and didn't even hesitate to accept. Well, he had learned three things that day: he could only ride five seconds with no hands, his momma was probably always right, and not being able to afford a good doctor can mean bad scaring—in this case, a ghastly scare on the side of his leg. He almost never wore shorts because of it. Few people had seen that scar. In fact, his own wife never saw him in a pair of shorts until after they were married. He knew at that point it didn't matter. He started thinking of clever names he could give Dr. Allen when he got back as a way of apologizing once again for seeming so cold. He said them aloud trying to hear which had the best ring to it.

"Dr. Super Suture. Dr. Snip and Clip. Dr. Invisa-Scar ..." The last one made him chuckle.

A gruff voice interrupted his superhero name assignment.

"What in tarnation are you talking about?" Sheriff Tate was grumbling.

Alford looked at his watch. Only thirty minutes left till the town meeting. "Sheriff, I'm so glad you're awake. Do you remember what happened?"

"Of course I do, boy," he said. "I'm not stupid, you know. I'll tell you all about it. First, I need you to help me sit up and get me off this silly table. I look like a popped can of biscuits on this thing. Second, I need a glass of water."

Alford was happy to oblige. At this point, if Sheriff Tate had asked him to stand on his head, he would have. He had to know what had happened so he could come up with a plan for the town, and he had to do it fast. He waited patiently as the sheriff chugged the water he'd been handed. Alford was doing his best not to be impatient, but he really needed to speed things along.

"Now, Sheriff," he began. "We actually have a town meeting we need to be getting to. The whole town is getting a little panicky, so I'd appreciate it if you could start at the beginning and tell me exactly what happened."

"Yes, I suppose they are," he answered. "I'm real sorry Mr. Newsome. It was a silly thing that happened, and I'm not even sure how it got so out of hand. I'm the sheriff for crying out loud, and I'm the reason the bar moved up."

He put his hands on his knees and then his head on his hands. He winced a little in pain, forgetting his arm was torn up.

Alford patted him on the back. "It's a shock to us all. I'm sure, whatever it was, that we can find a good solution. I can't do that, though, if you don't tell me what happened." Alford was trying his best to keep his voice calm and steady. He hadn't forgotten that Grayson was watching him back at Alpha on their monitoring chips.

Finally, the sheriff lifted his head. "Well, it all started after the ceremony," he began. "You did such a great job, and I was in the best mood. After all, we've been training and getting ready for this day for a while now. I'll be honest: I was sad at first to leave Alpha. We had made that our home, and it was comfortable. Not to mention the fact that, you know, impending death was no concern. After your speech, though, I looked around at all the smiling folks. The weather was nice, kids were laughing, parents were hugging, and there was nothing mean going on. It reminded me of the cause we all signed up for all those years ago, and I was inspired to do this. I drove around town for a little bit, just checking on things. I saw you at the market speaking to folks, and everything was going so well. I was happy. I went back to the station to make sure everything was in order, and that's when everything went bad. I pulled up to my spot, and that's when I heard it."

Alford interrupted. "The buzzard?" he asked in a high-pitched voice.

The sheriff looked as confused as Alford did.

"Sheriff, you said something about a stupid old buzzard to Charlie," Alford explained.

The sheriff began laughing. He laughed so hard that he started crying. This only added to Alford's confusion. He assumed there must still be some of the sedative in his body. He quieted his laughter after a few seconds and wiped a tear from his eye.

"Sorry, Mr. Newsome," the sheriff gasped. "I should explain. I call my patrol car, Old Buzzard. She was with me before the ReSet. We've seen many miles together. I was mad at the car. You see, as I put the car in park, I heard a loud bang. I'm not going to lie, I thought we were taking fire. Then, I remembered this was Utopian and not the world five years ago, so I knew that wasn't possible. I got out and realized that my back rear window had a gaping hole in it. The glass was cracked all around it. I couldn't believe my eyes. I must have hit a rock and somehow it ricocheted off something and went right through my window!"

"Whoa, Sherriff," Alford replied. "I'm confused though. Did you say something bad? How could a freak accident that you have no control over cause the Alpha team to move the bar up?"

"That's not the whole story," the sheriff continued. "I was so shaken, I shut my door to go inside and call you ... and realized I'd locked my keys in the car. They were still in the ignition! I was so frustrated, but I was being real careful not to do anything bad—control my temper. So, I had an idea. I would just carefully slide my arm through the hole and unlock the back door. Then I could climb in and get my keys. I was going to call you so you could come help me with the window."

"I'm still not seeing the issue here Sheriff," Alford said.

"There's more," he replied. "I don't know why I thought I could get my chubby arm through that hole. I was thinking that hole was bigger than it must have been. I was always really good playing that game Operation with my grandkids back before the ReSet, and I figured this was a piece of cake. Well, it wasn't. I sliced my arm all to bits. I got so stinking mad, and it hurt so bad that I took my steeled toe cowboy boot off and chunked it. Well, it hit the door to the Sherriff's station and shattered the window. That's when the alarm sounded and before I even realized what had come over me, it was too late. I'd just retrieved my shoe, cleaned out all the glass, and put it back when you pulled up."

"Oh, I see," Alford said.

"I'm really sorry," the sheriff said. "The whole thing was plum silly."

"Well, Sheriff, what's done is done," he replied. "I'm glad you weren't hurt worse. Now, we need to be united when we speak to the town. I need to step out there and tell David and Charlie what's going on. Then, I got about ten minutes to come up with a speech for that town meeting. You go ahead and compose yourself; I'm going to need you at your best for this meeting."

"I understand, and nothing like this will ever happen again," he said. "I promise." He extended his hand out to Alford.

Alford shook his hand and stepped out of the exam room, closing the door behind him. Immediately, Sheriff Tate's phone rang. He knew it was coming. He answered within three rings.

"That hurt more than I expected it to," he said. "Did I really have to cut my arm up for real, Jeffers?"

Not even acknowledging his whining, Grayson Jeffers began speaking. "Did he believe you?" he asked.

"Yes," the Sheriff replied. "Every word."

"Does he suspect anything?" Grayson added.

"Not a thing," Sheriff Tate replied.

"Good. I'll be in touch ..." and with that, Grayson Jeffers hung up the phone.

The sheriff looked to the corner of the exam room, nodded his head, and slipped his phone back into his pocket. He grabbed his hat that was sitting on the counter, put it on his head, began to whistle, and exited to meet up with Mr. Newsome.

TOWN HALL MEETING

Charlie had been sitting in the chair at the far side of the waiting room for what seemed like an eternity. Dr. Allen had been out of the room for almost thirty minutes. He was on his way out the door when David stopped him to talk. He wasn't intentionally eavesdropping but had heard enough of their conversation to know that he was as clueless as they were to the cause of the alarm. Charlie was grateful that since that first alarm, there hadn't been a second. He was concerned that the fear of the first mark happening this soon would cause hysteria among the people and that they would start slipping up and making mistakes. He wondered how his momma and Katie were holding up. He wondered if he had made the right choice coming to his father. His father had always told him, that he was to be the man of the house if he wasn't around. His momma had never liked that too much. He knew this because he had overheard them talking once before while he was trying to fall asleep. She told her father that it was too much pressure for a little boy and that he had already lost so much. He knew about the destruction of the world, but his family was amongst the chosen, so he knew at the very least that they hadn't lost their lives. So, he wasn't exactly sure what all he had lost, other than outside time. The way his mother had said it gave him the feeling there was more to the story. He wished his father would hurry. He could feel himself getting stressed and knew he needed to find a way to calm down. He stood up, put his hands on his head, and began to slowly walk around the waiting room. David noticed right away.

"Charlie, is it happening again?" David asked.

Charlie shook his head. This time, Dr. Allen started asking the questions.

"Is it the same level of pain as usual or worse?" he asked.

Charlie immediately felt his face begin to blush. He wasn't trying to be a source of attention. He hated when his heart did this. "The same, sir," he replied.

"Okay. Then I don't think we have a cause for concern just yet," Dr. Allen replied. "You let me know if it gets worse, though."

"Yes sir," Charlie replied.

David stopped Charlie from moving around and got down on one knee in front of him. He put his hand on Charlie's shoulder. "I know you, Char," he said. "You don't want to cause a scene—especially right now. We have to make sure you're okay. You know what the Alpha doctors said. Dr. Heathrow, the head of all the doctors, was very specific that if there is a change, it could be deadly, and we have to act on it right away. So please, it doesn't matter what is going on back there, if the pain is worse, you promise you would tell me the truth?"

Charlie was grateful that David was at the clinic with them. He knew eventually he would be headed back to Alpha, but for now, he was there, and it relieved Charlie.

"Yes, sir. I will," Charlie answered. "It's the same right now, though. I'll just do my breathing exercises and should be fine. I promise to tell you if something changes."

"That a boy!" David said, rising to his feet and going back to speak with Dr. Allen.

Charlie was a little shocked that David believed him. Not that he was trying to deceive him—because he had no intention of lying to anybody—but a part of him knew that even if his chest pain was worse, he would be too terrified to mention it at a time like this.

He continued his breathing exercises and hoped that it wouldn't get worse, so he wouldn't have to face that predicament. Charlie had an incident at his K/5 initiation that had never happened before, and the team at Alpha was very careful not to duplicate it. Every person's chip location was randomly selected. The head chairs weren't even allowed to know where their own families were. Everything was entered into the Alpha mainframe that was security encrypted and only Grayson had the password for it. However, something had gone wrong with Charlie's implant. The only location that they weren't supposed to implant was the heart, or close to the heart. Charlie's selected location the was top of the liver. When Dr. Heathrow was attempting the implant, Charlie had a reaction to the anesthesia and began crashing. A team of medical staff rushed to help, but there wasn't enough of them. Every person was doing the jobs of two people. Dr. Heathrow had insisted that they not chip him right then. Grayson Jeffers had overseen every implant and he objected to the delay. He had said that it was clear the boy wouldn't be able to handle being put under anesthesia a second time around, so it had to be right now while they were already in. Dr. Heathrow had paused, momentarily thinking over what had just been said. He took a step back toward the still-fading Charlie and looked at him closely. He knew in his heart the implant was a risk he wasn't willing to take. This was a bad idea. He had told Grayson he couldn't do it. He told Grayson that it was better that Charlie never be chipped than risk doing something so dangerous while he was crashing. Grayson had given him a death stare that could have woken the dead, but he ignored his glare and went back to the mission of rescuing Charlie.

Grayson was furious and remarked that it always came down to him to get things done. He grabbed the thin metal tubing that was used to place the implants, walked over to the operating table, and before Dr. Heathrow even realized what was happening, shoved it into Charlie's open body. Grayson had done several impromptu medical tasks on the fields in the middle of wars and had seen Dr. Heathrow do these implants hundreds of times, so he was confident he could handle it. Sadly, he was too confident. He had accidentally shoved the implant tube too far and the chip had gone straight into Charlie's heart. There was a rip in in his right ventricle and Charlie immediately began bleeding. Grayson had taken a step back, and it was visible on his face that he had made a terrible mistake. Dr. Heathrow had yelled at him and quickly reacted to the now excessive blood loss.

Charlie's vitals were dropping even faster than they had been before, and it looked very bleak. Grayson stood back and watched as Charlie's tiny body lay near lifeless on the operating table. He watched as his team worked frantically to rescue the five-year-old. He had never admitted it, but he felt as if he might throw up. He was lost in thought when the eerie sound of the flatline interrupted his thoughts. He looked at the monitor and realized that Charlie was dying. Dr. Heathrow hurriedly grabbed the paddles and began to shock Charlie. He did this three different times before a faint beeping sound on the monitor made the entire room erupt in applause. Dr. Heathrow spent the next thirty minutes getting Charlie back and stitching him up. However, he was not able to retrieve or relocate the chip. After several hours of recovery, it was explained to Charlie's parents what had happened, with one key piece of information omitted. Grayson Jeffers had threatened everyone in that room that if they were to tell anybody that it was he who had made the mistake, their entire families would pay the price. He didn't say exactly what he would do, but people knew enough not to question it. Dr. Heathrow took the blame for the implant. Charlie's parents were very understanding and were more concerned about the aftermath. It was explained that the implant constantly sent signals to the nanobots by using the body's natural electric charge. The fear that it being in his heart caused was that there was a chance that when the chip was sending out the signal, it would interfere with the heart's rhythm and send Charlie into cardiac failure. There was also an almost guarantee that Charlie would experience chest pains at different times in his life. That would be normal, but they had to make sure his heart didn't get too elevated or the pain didn't get too extreme. They were cautioned that at the first signs that this could be happening, they should send a distress call to Alpha and have him flown out to Dr. Heathrow. His parents were grateful to Dr. Heathrow for saving him, and both hugged his neck. Dr. Heathrow was angry that he was hiding the truth from them. What choice did he have?

Now, as Charlie paced through the waiting room, he wondered if this would be the time his heart gave out. He lived with this thought every time this happened but didn't dare tell his parents because he didn't want to cause them undue stress. It seemed as if the breathing exercises Dr. Heathrow had taught him helped quite a bit, and luckily, he had never needed any further medical attention. He could feel the chest pain lessening and decided to sit down again. He took his original seat at the back of the waiting room and looked at the clock. The town meeting would be starting soon. Where was his father?

That's when something caught Charlie's attention. He looked at David, who was talking once again to Dr. Allen. He didn't see him moving his hand toward his pocket, so he knew he must be confused. He could have sworn he heard the faint sound of the specific ringtone Grayson Jeffers had for the head chairs. Without giving him much time to ponder that thought, his father came from the back. He was so happy to see him that he jumped to hug him. It must have been his phone ringing. Then, why wasn't he on it? The thought quickly entered Charlie's mind.

"Son, did you have another episode?" his father asked.

Charlie still hadn't figured out how his dad always knew. Charlie shook his head and leaned against his dad's arm. "Yes, sir, but it wasn't a bad one, and I'm all right."

"I made sure it was a normal one, Al," David said. "Did you find out what happened?"

"Yes, I did," he replied. "It isn't a serious deal other than the fact we got a mark against us. I have to gather my thoughts as we head over to the town meeting. You mind giving us all a lift?"

“Sure,” David replied. “Where’s Sheriff Tate?”

“I’m right here,” the sheriff said, coming from the back. “I’m sorry, fellas, this is all my fault.”

The men in the room didn’t know how to respond. There was an awkward silence that filled the room, which Charlie didn’t handle very well.

“Sheriff,” Charlie interrupted. “We forgive you. I know we all have to be really well-behaved. I know we all don’t want a mark to happen. But we all know one or two will, so we’ll just let Father deal with it, and everything will be okay. You’ll see.”

The sheriff looked upset by Charlie’s words and Charlie instantly regretted speaking. He closed one eye, waiting for another alarm to sound, in case Grayson took that as speaking out of place.

The sheriff seemed to recognize Charlie’s concern and walked over and put his arm around his shoulders. “I appreciate that, boy,” he said. “Those are some mighty big words for someone so young. Maybe you should be the sheriff,” he said with a chuckle. “I also heard you took good care of me while I was zonked out. Dr. Allen better watch out or he may be out of a job, too.”

At that, everyone laughed, and the awkwardness disappeared from the room.

“We have two minutes. Let’s go,” Alford said. All the men filed out of the clinic and piled into David’s truck. They went the three blocks back to the town square where, what now seemed like ages ago, they had just welcomed everyone to the city. The entire town was already in its place. The men got out of their truck and took their place in the crowd. Alford went to his wife, gave her a reassuring squeeze on her hand, and mounted the platform. The whole town shushed in unison to hear what was going on. Alford closed his eyes for a moment, took a deep breath, and then opened his eyes to begin.

“Citizens of Utopian,” he began, “it is with a heavy heart that we are meeting here right now. This was not a drill, nor was this part of the plan. I take the leadership of this town very seriously, which is why I’m so burdened by the fact that we already have a mark against us. Please, take this time and look at that bar. I know it doesn't seem like it right now, but one mark against us is not a good thing—especially on day one. I know the majority of you are probably wondering why I'm not sounding so optimistic right now. I know you're probably hoping for positive affirmations. Well, I do want to offer you hope, but I also want to offer you the truth. The truth is, we have to be careful. The truth is, we have to be mindful. The truth is, we have to be good. Our way of life depends on it. Sheriff Tate is in the audience with us, and he will be the first to tell you that what happened today was silly and should not have taken place. He had a series of bad events that happened to him, but ultimately, he let it get the best of him, and not only did he raise the bar—he was injured in the process. Now, I do not want anyone treating our sheriff differently because of this. He knows how serious this is and he is deeply bothered by his actions. He has asked for public forgiveness, which we will all provide him because it's what is right. The truth is, I'm happy this happened."

Alford could hear gasps fill across the audience. He saw the confusion and his own wife's face. He knew he needed to explain before there was a mutiny.

"Let me explain," he said. "I'm happy this happened because it has made us realize that this is not a game. This is serious. We've all lived through the simulations; we've all read the plans; and we've all been vetted by Mr. Jeffers. However, we hadn't had a real experience. Well, this was that. I'm glad we got that out of the way to start. So, if any of you had any doubts about the vision and the mission, you have been corrected. Let this be an example, proving that we cannot afford to make foolish decisions. Let this also be a reminder that we are all in this together and we rely on each other. We literally need each other to survive. So, let's learn from this. Let's grow from this. Most importantly, let's remain Utopian United."

WE MADE IT

Katie looked at herself in the mirror as her momma fussed over her dress. "Momma, did you turn my chip off?" she asked.

Her mother nodded her head. "Yes, dear."

"Did you turn it off for a long time or just the normal time?" Katie asked again.

Her mother stopped fussing and rested her head on Katie's shoulder, producing the image of both of them in the mirror together. Katie always loved looking at her momma. She was so beautiful. She wished she had taken after her momma instead of her father. It was weird to look like her father, but it's not like she had a say in what her face would look like. Katie rested her head on her mother's head, and they just sat in silence staring. She knew her mother was going to give a speech any second, but she wanted to enjoy this moment just a little longer. Her mother lifted her head and turned her to face her. She scooped her in her lap and rubbed her back.

"Katie," she began. "You needn't worry about the time of the chips, dear. That's for us to worry about, but I'll explain it one more time. If our family needs extra time, your father has our code to the system, and he can log in and shut our chips off—well, except for your brother's. Charlie's goes non-stop. However, your dad can enter a special code and it puts a firewall around his chip. The feed doesn't stop, but instead, it sends the signal to satellites all over the world. This delays the feed to Team Alpha. It only gives Charlie a thirty-minute blackout, but it makes Charlie feel like the rest of us. Grayson has told each member that when the signal is buffering, this is what's going on and there's no need to worry about keeping up with the feed, especially if the rest of the family's feed is dark. It's kinda like a backdoor to going dark. We don't do this very often, but it is available to us if we need it. You know how your father feels about this, though. He wants us to live like everyone else in Utopian lives. So, Mr. Jeffers has given everyone access in their homes for their chips to be shut off temporarily for privacy. When we scan our hands outside our bedroom and bathroom, we get ten minutes. If we're going to bed or taking a nap, we can scan our hand twice and we get all the time we need for rest until we scan again, as long as the bed monitors pick up our body in the bed and can tell we are at a resting heart rate. That is why Mr. Jeffers has called your father so many times over the last five years—because Charlie's heart sometimes beats faster than it should, even while he's sleeping. So, I know you worry about the times that our chips are shut off, but it isn't a problem, my love. Today is a day for celebrating, not worrying."

She kissed Katie's forehead and sighed. "Oh dear, I got lipstick all over you again. I always tell myself to be careful with these kisses, but I just can't help it! Let's go. Our time is actually almost up, and we need to reactivate our chips. I'll do your hair in the living room. We must hurry. We can't be late for the celebration!"

They stepped out of Katie's bedroom together, and each scanned their individual hands. Mother rushed over to the counter and grabbed a paper towel. She wet it and came back to where Katie was sitting and started wiping the lipstick off. She threw the towel away and guided her daughter to the living room. She motioned for her to sit on the floor while she sat on the couch. She parted her hair down the middle, ready to begin the double French braids her daughter loved so much.

"Will you pretty please with sugar on top put ribbons into the braids this time, Momma?" Katie asked.

"I planned to, sweetie. This is a big day, so we want to look our absolute best," Momma said.

"Can I have big bows at the end too?" she asked.

Momma nodded her head and smiled. "Now, sit still so I can get them perfect," she said.

"Yes, ma'am. I'm so excited. I can't wait to show Father. He's going to love my hair like this!" said Katie, nearly squealing the last few words.

The two sat in silence for just a few moments. Beth loved braiding her daughter's hair because it gave her quality time that was just the two of them. Sometimes, it was just a quick ponytail, but sometimes she tried elaborate styles that took her at least thirty minutes. No matter how long each one took, she always loved the time it provided. Katie was a surprise baby that they weren't planning on. After everything they had been through, they had determined that just having Charlie was enough for them. Even when they had signed up for this mission, they had no plans for another child. In fact, Grayson had made it pretty clear that he didn't want to add new bodies until everyone was established in their new cities—unless you were going to remain at Alpha and not enter one of the cities. Beth and Alford were fine with that, too. They were content being the three amigos.

However, as they entered the year of ReSet, the unexpected happened. When they joined the Alpha Project, Charlie was two years old. They joined with the rest of the chairs that Grayson had selected, and together they scoured all the people that Grayson had selected, trying to narrow it down to the people who would be the remaining five hundred people in the world. This was not an easy task. They could not believe the amount of work that Grayson had already done. He had already selected what he considered to be the top ten thousand people in the world who were still moral and good. He had created an algorithm that allowed him to enter certain key aspects and character traits of people, as well as achievements, and run it to find these people. The US had moved into such a technological era that everyone was forced to basically live out their lives on a social platform. Nobody was exempt. Every citizen of the US was logged into a government database called the Freedom Census. It was said that this was created to make sure that the government could protect every American, at all times. At birth, hospitals entered you into the system via your social security number, and it was up to you to keep it personally updated, or you received a $20,000 fine at the end of the year with your tax return. Nobody had ever forgotten to log themselves. The government knew that if you wanted something from the American people, you had to go after their wallets first. The workforce used it to log new employees, and they kept a record of every call-in, tardy, work complaint, work commendation, and so forth into this mainframe. Businesses used it to log disruptive customers, educational facilities used it to log every disciplinary action and academic achievement, the police departments used it to log every offense and act of heroism, and newspapers used it when they covered good and bad media.

Grayson was able to manipulate that system with his algorithm to find the best subjects left in America. Now, they were tasked with narrowing down the ten thousand and sorting them into the key cities. After that was the hardest part. Even though they knew about it ahead of time, nothing could have prepared them for what was to happen next. The destruction of mankind.

Beth still had nightmares, the screams filling her brain as she tried to sleep. It was one of those nights when she couldn't sleep that she began to sob uncontrollably. She had accidentally woken Alford. He tried his best to comfort her, but he too was having a hard time dealing with the emotions of the death they had aided in. A month later, they realized they were pregnant with Katie. Jeffers was furious at first but said he would make an exception since they were chairs. Beth had feared bringing a child into the middle of the New World ReOrder, but Katie had been an absolute joy. She was full of life and sass, which they had to watch closely. She marched to the beat of her own drum. Her strawberry-blonde hair, the one trait she had inherited from her mother, trailed her back and was straight as a board. She had insisted that it never be cut. She had once said that she wanted hair so long she could tie it to a tree and make her very own swing anytime she wanted. While Charlie was easygoing and calm, Katie was a fireball. Their children balanced each other perfectly.

"Momma," Katie began again.

Mother smiled. Her daughter's mind was always working. There was never a moment when she wasn't asking a question. This had been hard at times for Beth because it truly tested her patience. She had gotten a mark once before. Katie had been talking ninety miles a minute, and Beth already felt unwell. Her daughter was going on and on about a caterpillar she had found in the garden and how she wanted to keep it. Beth's head was pounding so badly, and she just wasn't thinking clearly.

"Shut up!" she yelled. "Please, for once, just stop talking."

It happened at the same time. Beth heard the alarm go off outside, and her daughter's eyes filled with tears. With a trembling voice, she said, "Yes ma'am" and asked to be excused to her room. Her mother had told her no, grabbed her in a hug, and apologized. She had explained how bad she felt. Of course, Katie had forgiven her, but since that day, Beth had to watch how she reacted to Katie. She had used one of her techniques from the class she taught. She wore a rubber band on her arm, and when she felt her patience slipping, she popped the thin, cold rubber to help her mind focus on the action instead.

"Yes, dear?" she answered her daughter again.

"I was thinking," Katie began. "You know, it's been four years since my initiation and getting my chip." You know how two years ago, I got mad at Charlie and called him a booger butt?" Her eyes widened and she cupped her hands over her mouth. She fearfully looked up at her mother.

"You weren't calling anyone that this time, sweetie. You can't get a mark for it," her mother said.

She slowly removed her hands from her mouth. She paused a moment and began again. "You know how the next year I took that money out of your purse, and then at school, I looked at Mary Ellen's paper and wrote her answer, and then I knocked over your lamp and it broke and I lied to you, and then I ..."

Beth could feel her impatience climbing. They had to get to the town square, and she didn't have time for a "Katie Tale". She popped her rubber band three times and took a deep breath. "Katie, is there a point to this?" Mother asked sweetly. "I remember each time you did those things, the bar went up, remember?"

"Yes ma'am. I was just curious how you and Father knew those things, even when all those people didn't tattle on me."

Mother chuckled. "Your mind is always working, and I love that about you. Well sweetie, since your father is the head chair of this city, he gets a daily report of all the reasons the bar went up. He sees the citizen's name and the incident. Then, your dad meets with those individuals and tries to work with them on how to make better choices the next time they find themselves in those situations."

"Is that why we have all those classes we go to?" Katie asked.

"Mm-hmm," mother replied. "We host those classes, so we can all grow together and learn how to be the best we can be. We're trying to make the world good again. That is the mission and that is the dream. We should be proud of ourselves. We have done a really great job."

"How come you've never talked to Charlie about his incidents?" Katie asked.

"Well, your bubba has never done anything to get a mark," her mother explained.

Katie turned her head slowly to meet her mother's gaze. Her baby blue eyes widened again. "What in the world!" she said. "Not one thing?"

Her mother slowly turned her head back and continued the braid. "Not one thing."

"How does he do that?" Katie asked.

"I have no idea," her mother said. "Your bubba has always just been very good at being very good. He works very hard to make sure he never does anything wrong. I think every citizen has had at least one mark, and although we made it to our five-year anniversary with only 63 percent of the bar filled, your brother is the only one who hasn't added to that percentage. Now, we don't discuss these things with the Utopianites, young lady; this is a private discussion. We never tell anyone who makes the marks; we don't want anyone bullying anybody. Do you understand?"

Katie smiled, lifted her fingers to her lips, and pretended as if she was zipping them up.

"There, done!" her mother said as she patted the top of Katie's head.

"May, I go look?" Katie asked.

"Quickly," Momma replied. "It is almost time."

Katie ran to her bedroom, and her squeal filled the house. "Father is going to love this! Thank you, Momma!" she said out loud.

"You're welcome, love. Now, let's go," her mother said.

Katie ran back to the living room and grabbed her mother's hand. Momma twirled Katie around, which made her giggle. They opened the door and stepped outside. Standing on the hill, overlooking the city, they could see that everyone was making their way to the town square. Five years had come and gone pretty quickly, and the city of Utopian was doing excellent. Her husband was constantly trying to improve the quality of life and was so good at teaching everyone new techniques on how to handle anything negative that might come their way. She was so proud to be married to him. The thought warmed her to the core.

The city was buzzing with music. The platform was in its place and decorated with red, white, and blue silk ribbons and banners. No doubt an attempt to impress Grayson, she thought as she rolled her eyes. She looked at her watch and realized if they didn't move quickly, they would be late. As they headed down the hill and got closer to town, she thought of everything that had brought them to this point, and she was so pleased. Utopian was home and these people had all become family. They had two families who each had a new baby in the last year. After so much death for so long, they were growing, thriving, and creating a New World that was really surrounded by a lot of good. Finally, Grayson's plan was coming together, and she was so happy they had gotten on board in the very beginning. They had already made it to the square and immediately spotted Charlie. He was standing by the willow.

"Charlie, is everything okay?" asked Mother.

He turned to look at her. She couldn't believe how old he looked. They had just celebrated his thirteenth birthday only a few months back, but he looked closer to sixteen. She didn't think it was possible, but he seemed to have gained more freckles over those last few months. He walked over to where she was standing and kissed her on the cheek. Then, he kissed Katie on the forehead.

"Yes ma'am," he said. "I was just staring at the Willow. I can't believe how big it's gotten in the last five years; it's pretty impressive."

"So, are you, Bubba," Katie said.

Charlie twisted his face in confusion.

"Don't worry, it's our secret. Right, Momma?" Katie asked.

Charlie still looked confused.

"Don't worry, Char," his mother said. "I'll explain later. Right now, it's time to start."

He shook his head, grabbed his sister's hand, and the three of them headed to their seats on the platform. Mick and Sal came to the platform with trumpets. They raised them at the same time and played a verse of "Amazing Grace". Charlie had no idea that Mr. Mick and Mr. Sal were even able to play an instrument. He figured they must have been working on it specially for today's celebration. These were two of Charlie's favorite people to be around. They had served in the military together, and Sal had received a purple heart for pulling Mick out after he took fire and went unconscious in the middle of a war. Years later, Sal got renal cancer and Mick donated a kidney to save his life. These two had spent their whole lives protecting their country and each other so it was a no-brainer for the team to spare their lives for the New World and to keep them together. They both taught in the small Utopian school. The entire town applauded as the two men fist-bumped each other and then took their seats.

Alford then stepped forward. Charlie was so busy watching Mick and Sal that he hadn't seen where his father came from. He had been waiting to see him all day.

"Utopianites, I want you to give a warm welcome, to the reason we are all alive and well today, Mr. Grayson Jeffers. He is here very briefly, and he has a surprise for us all," Alford said.

Grayson Jeffers stepped onto the platform from the audience. Charlie didn't even know he was coming, no doubt Jeffers' idea. The crowd hushed and you could feel the shift in the atmosphere.

"I am pleased with all your progress," Grayson said dryly. "I know, at times, it has seemed scary, but you've pulled it off. As promised, I have a surprise for you—actually two. The first is we will now ReFresh your behavior bar. Every five years that you make it without reaching the top of the bar, you will get another ReFresh to your bar. Also, as you go to the park later, you will now see on the lamp posts new signs that say, 'UTOPIAN: SOMEONE IS ALWAYS WATCHING.' These signs are meant to be a reminder of two things. You made it once; you can do it again—and that we have not stopped watching. So, with that, keep up the good work, and hopefully, I will see you all alive in five years. Newsome, back to you."

With that, he exited the platform, went straight to a black four-door jeep that was parked near the willow, got in, and sped off.

It seemed as if the entire town was holding its breath until he left. Alford got back up next. "Mr. Grayson Jeffers, ladies and gentlemen. Now, let me say, I'm so proud of each of you. It has been five years, and yes, we have made mistakes, but we have learned and will continue to learn from them. So, let's enjoy this time of celebration. We have food and a great evening of fun lined up. So, there is nothing left to say except, Utopian, we made it!"

PHOENIX

~ *Risen from the Ashes*

A year had come and gone since Utopian celebrated its five-year mark. Alford was so proud of his town. They had overcome so much, and the hard work had finally paid off. They had proven that they could do it. They could go five years without hitting 100 percent on the behavior bar. They proved that this town could make it. Since their town was successful, Grayson had decided to go ahead and start two more. The original plan was to space them out, but he was confident that they had a good blueprint for success after monitoring Utopian for five years. He asked Alford to join Bo in Phoenix for their opening day. He was sending David to Evermore to meet up with Slate. Alford thought the idea of separating him and David was wise. He couldn't put his finger on it, but David was acting strangely. However, Alford also thought that Sheriff Tate was acting strangely, too. David was stationed at Alpha, but it seemed as if David had been around more in the last year than he had been in the first five. He also seemed to come into town and have clandestine meetings with the sheriff. He didn't have any proof, but every time Alford would happen to walk in on any of these secret meetings, the conversation would hush, and the men looked as if they were caught doing something illegal. Alford had pulled David to the side to confront him, but David had just blown it off and told him to stop acting paranoid. Alford wanted to believe him, but he noticed he bit his lip when he said it. He knew something was up, but he needed more concrete evidence before accusing his best friend of anything. At this point, he didn't even have anything to accuse him of. He had hoped he could do some investigating while the two of them were apart. He had also put his best agent, Charlie, on the case. He had instructed Charlie to pay attention to the sheriff's movements while he was away and report anything unusual to his father when he arrived back.

Charlie had panicked at first when his father was speaking. His father had consoled him and told him that he had entered the delay code and the blackout code for their conversation. He reminded Charlie that Alpha didn't pay much attention to them while they were all down because they were the chair family, so they got special privileges. Even though his father seemed calm, Charlie had felt uneasy inside because he knew his father didn't like participating in those "special privileges".

"I don't know what I'm going to do without you for two days, Mr. Newsome," Beth said as she wrapped her arms around her husband's neck and showered him in kisses.

"Ewww, Yuck!" Katie said. "I know you two are married and all, but we are your kids, and we don't want to see that you know." She stepped into the yard and bent over, acting as if she were about to lose her lunch.

"Oh K.K., stop being so silly," Charlie said as he loaded his father's duffel bag into the trunk of the car and slammed it shut.

His parents were still hugging and kissing.

"On second thought," Charlie said as he picked his sister up and spun her around. "I'm with her. Come on, guys. That's enough love for one day," he teased.

"Well, that's too bad," Father began. "I was saving some for my kids, but I guess they don't need it," he said as he casually began walking to his car.

Katie wiggled free from her brother and took off in a mad dash. "Wait!" she hollered. "Please don't leave without a kiss, Father!"

He froze where he was standing and waited until her footsteps got closer. He spun around and scooped her up, squeezing her tightly. "I would never, Katie-Bug!"

"Anaconda Squeeze," she said as she returned her own squeeze. She loved her father so much.

He set her down. "Be a big help to momma while I'm away. Remember your manners, and do all your schoolwork without any trouble," he ordered.

She extended her small pinky and waited patiently for her father to return his. "Pinky promise," she said as they intertwined pinkies.

He patted her twice on the butt and motioned her toward her mother. Charlie walked his father to the car. Without even realizing it was happening, his eyes began to fill with tears. He was completely caught off guard and embarrassed by his reactions. His pale freckled face began to turn red, and he turned his face from his father. Ever since they had left Alpha, he had been by his father's side for some of the hardest things to face at Utopian, and he was just now realizing the gravity of his father leaving. He was worried something bad would happen to the city while he was away.

"Hey, kiddo," his father began. "It's okay to feel sad about me leaving; you're allowed to have emotions."

"No, sir," Charlie replied. "It's not just that."

His father looked confused. "Well, what else is it?"

"Father, what if something terrible happens while you're gone?" Charlie asked. "What if mass chaos erupts and everyone starts doing bad things. What if the whole town joins in and the behavior bar starts climbing? What if because you're gone people lose hope and go crazy? What if we have to go into ReSet and Mr. Jeffers kills the town, and you aren't here ..."

"Whoa, Whoa, Whoa," Father interrupted. "Slow down, Champ. You put too much on your shoulders, and I'm sorry because I feel like I'm part to blame for that. Everything is going to be just fine. The sheriff is here. Mick and Sal are also aware of what to do if things happen. Momma has the code to access the daily log, and she has instructions on what to do if something needs to be addressed. Buddy, we've done well for six years now. Nothing is going to happen over the next three days. You'll see."

"I really would like to go with you," Charlie said, trying hard to stop his lip from quivering.

"I would love that too, Son," his father said. "I need you to stay here, though. Grayson didn't approve you to travel this time."

Charlie dropped his head in disappointment.

"Don't forget, though: you have that special project you're working on!" his father said.

Charlie immediately raised his, his eyes now sparkling with determination. He had almost forgotten. His father needed him for a very important job. "I'll make a great grade on it, Father," he said as he winked.

His father smiled so wide that almost all of his teeth were showing. "I know you will," he said, winking back. Then, he hugged Charlie and kissed the top of his head.

Charlie walked over to join his sister and mother.

Father got into the car and shut the door. He slowly began backing down the driveway while his family waved to him. They continued to wave until he could no longer see them down the hill. He too felt his eyes getting wet; he had no desire to leave them or Utopian. He said a quick prayer that everything would be just fine. If he didn't stop, he could get to Phoenix in six hours, but he had been overworked lately and was extremely tired. He had plans to stop in a destroyed city on the way and just rest in his car for a few hours. Beth had prepared him a full meal for dinner and lots of snacks. He didn't mind driving. It had been a huge part of his former life. He was a computer genius and had worked for a medical research facility. They were trying to find cures for terminal illnesses. He was in charge of "all things computer". He was also tasked with traveling between the three facilities that his boss owned. Each facility was several hours from the next. In his spare time, he volunteered as a designated driver in Beth's programs. Driving allowed him the freedom to think clearly and separate from the everyday stresses of life. If he was being honest, this was the one reason he was looking forward to the drive. He was also excited to see Bo. It had been over six years since he and Bo Billings had enjoyed a meal together, and he was looking forward to some famous "Bo's Blazing Brisket".

Bo Billings was as nice as they came. He was a redneck, and he was proud of it. He was very young when Grayson met him, but he had already accomplished more with his life than most ever did. Bo's father was a deadbeat who had suddenly lost interest in Bo's momma as soon as she told him she was pregnant, and sadly Bo's momma only had one interest—drugs. He bounced around between foster homes and boys' homes his entire young life. He never caused any trouble, but as he grew, the chances of a foster family adopting him diminished exponentially. A loving family eventually adopted him when he was fourteen. Sadly, he had already lost his childhood. He was eternally grateful to his adopted parents and treated them as if they were his biological family. As soon as Bo turned eighteen and finished school, he started a non-profit called "Rodeo Rescue". Bo ran a rodeo camp for all foster and orphaned children. He taught them all there was to know about rodeos, cowboys, hard work, and respect. Most importantly, he showed them love. He worked hand in hand with foster-care agencies to help take a more proactive approach in training and helping to create more foster homes, encouraging people to take in and adopt foster kids. Through his hard work, in his first three years working at his non-profit, he helped to place over 250 kids into their new forever homes. He also made a personal commitment to never marry because he didn't want anything to take his focus from the cause. He had a hard time when Grayson approached him because he couldn't come to grips with that many children losing their lives. It took Grayson several meetings to convince him his plan was actually helping children in the long run.

Grayson finally twisted Bo's thinking and won him over. Grayson explained how all the children that Bo was trying to help were only in that position because of bad parents. With Grayson's plan, there would never be bad parents again. Everyone would be starting off as great people who were all trying to create a great world, just as Bo was attempting. After several more conversations, Bo was finally on board, with one exception. He insisted that his adoptive parents come too. Grayson objected at first. Although he said they weren't necessarily "bad" people, they didn't quite make the percentages needed to make it to the selection round. Bo politely shook Grayson's hand and said no thank you. He informed Grayson he was good to go down in flames with everyone else after he outed Grayson to the press. Before Bo was able to fully exit the BBQ joint they were having lunch in, Grayson halted him. He didn't take too kindly to threats, but Bo was someone he was very interested in. He had plans for Bo Billings, and he was willing to make an exception.

With Bo's parents on board, Bo signed up for the ReSet. Alford had first met Bo right before their first chair meeting. Charlie had fallen and scraped his knee. Before Alford could get to him, Bo was there. He apologized for leaving his dollar bill on the floor and allowing Charlie to trip on it. Charlie looked down and didn't see anything and looked back up at Bo. He had now stopped crying because he hadn't seen any money and was very confused about what this man was talking about. Bo put his hand behind his ear and when he brought it back, he had a dollar bill in his hand. He begged Charlie to keep it for all the trouble and asked Charlie to forgive him. Alford had stopped to watch this entire encounter with this stranger and his son. Charlie, still dumbfounded, agreed, shook Bo's hand, and slowly walked away no longer aware that his knee hurt.

As Alford approached to thank him, Bo interrupted his thoughts.

"No need to thank me, sir. You got a great boy there. I was happy to help. Name's Bo. Bo Billings," he said.

Alford extended his hand for a shake and wasn't prepared for what happened next. Bo wrapped his burly arms around him, picked him up, shook him a few times, and set him back down.

"No can do with the shakey-shakey. I hug family, and the way I see it, we're all about to be real close, wouldn't you agree?" he asked.

Alford chuckled quietly at first and then broke into a full laugh. Bo just stared at him. After a few seconds, Alford composed himself. "I'm sorry, Mr. Billings. I just wasn't expecting anything of that sort. Especially not from a stranger," he replied. "I do, however, so appreciate what you did for my Charlie. I would love to take you to lunch one day to repay your kindness."

Bo flashed him a smile, revealing that he was missing his front left tooth. "I'll do you one better. I'll make you some brisket. It'll change your life."

In that moment, Alford wanted two things: to ask what in the world had happened to that man's tooth and to taste brisket that would change his life. "I say, that sounds like a plan, Mr. Billings," he replied.

"We family now, member? Call me Bo," he replied.

"Okay, Bo, and I'm Alford Newsome," Alford replied.

"You good with Al?" Bo asked. "I like Al."

Al nodded his head. "Works for me, Bo. Let's get to that meeting," he replied.

Alford's stomach grumbled as he continued down the road. He knew that whatever Beth made would be delicious, but even she knew there was nothing as good as "Bo's Blazing Brisket". He turned the radio on and was met with constant static. He couldn't believe he had made such a rookie mistake. There were no more broadcasting stations. He shut it off and continued his journey. As anticipated the hum of the car, the road beneath him, and a lack of radio added to his exhaustion and he had to pull over to take a quick nap.

Upon waking, he finished his journey rolling into Phoenix right around noon, and as soon as he crossed into town, a familiar face brought a smile to his face. He slowed the car and came to a complete stop as Bo slapped the hood of his car.

"Wowee, if it ain't Mr. Success himself," Bo hollered. He ran to the driver's side door and flung it open. He practically pulled Alford's arm off getting him out of the car. Then, he recreated that very first hug. This time, however, when Bo put him down, Alford returned the same gesture which sent Bo into a laughing fit.

"I'm more tickled than a pig wearing a pink dress on a sunshiny day in a mud pit during feed time," Bo said.

Alford knew nothing of what interested a pig, and he was confident that pigs didn't wear dresses of any color, but he knew enough to know that Bo was excited. "It's great to see you too, Bo!" Alford replied. "Are you ready for today? Do you have any questions?"

"One very important question," Bo said as his face grew serious. "You hungry?" he asked.

Alford smiled and nodded his head, hoping that meant there was brisket waiting.

"Good!" Bo replied. "Follow me down to my house, and I'll feed you real good before we get this shindig kicked off."

Alford chuckled out loud and got back in his car. He was happier to see Bo and to get out of Utopian for a few days than he thought he would be. He followed Bo in his black-on-black Ford F150 as they traveled through the town. Phoenix was different than Alford had remembered. It was more countryside and farmland, but he knew that was fitting for Bo. He pulled up to Bo's house after a ten-minute drive and wasn't shocked at all. Bo's house looked exactly like a barn. It was pale yellow with white "X" doors, and there was even a weathervane with a metal rooster on top of the house.

Alford stepped inside, and the smell of leather and cedar filled his nose. This cabin screamed Bo Billings! It was masculine yet inviting. Another smell—this one familiar—hit Alford all at once, and his stomach echoed in response. Bo had indeed smoked some brisket, and Alford was elated. The two sat down and caught up. Bo had been asked to help do some of the monitoring of the town to see how Alford was getting things done. Bo said that, for him, it hadn't been like six years because he saw Al at least once a week. The comment made Alford uneasy. He always knew they were being watched, but hearing someone actually say it didn't sit well with him, and he wondered why it bothered him so much. Bo talked about what he had been up to with creating the town and how he was excited to incorporate some of the things he loved as well. He had convinced Grayson to let him start a rodeo in the town and allow the kids to be involved. Bo was as full of life—as he had always been. After lunch, he showed Alford his property. It truly was breathtaking. If Alford hadn't been a part of the destruction in this very town, you wouldn't have been able to convince him that anything terrible had happened here. The only time Bo's demeanor changed was when he stopped beside two little white crosses at the far end of his property. He told Alford he wasn't ready to talk about it and moved on very quickly. Alford made a mental note to check into it.

The men went to the celebration as planned and had an initiation very similar to Utopians. However, in true Bo fashion, he didn't plant a willow. In fact, he didn't plant anything. Instead, he had a full-size bronzed bull statue erected in his town square. When he revealed it, Alford almost spit out the water he had just taken a drink of.

Bo went on to explain to the town that, like the bull, he wanted their town to be strong in the face of adversity and to withstand any obstacle that came their way. He wanted them to take on this mission with tenacity and determination. He encouraged his town to "be the bull". The town seemed to understand exactly what he meant because they met his challenge with a hearty "yee-haw", in unison. No doubt, Bo Billings had become the heartbeat of this town, and Alford couldn't have been prouder of his friend.

Alford sat back and watched this hillbilly, full of life, motivate a group of people to be wild animals, and they loved it. Alford had juggled this new way of life in his head often, but in this moment, he was back in full support of Grayson's vision. His town had survived, and he had no doubt, that with Bo leading this group, they would too. Alford truly believed that in fifty years, even if he wasn't alive to see it, the world would be on track to once again being good and full of life. The thought warmed his heart. The meeting ended, and Bo invited the whole town to the city hall for a celebration dinner and line dancing. He even convinced Alford to come for a few hours before hitting the road.

"I'm proud of you, Bo," Alford said. "You did a really great job with your people back there."

"Thanks, Brother," Bo replied, slapping Alford on the back three times. "I've learned a thing or two from you, truth be told."

The two men sat down at the main table and spent the next couple of hours enjoying the music, food, and fellowship of all the Phoenix people. Alford knew them all and it was nice to catch up with old friends. It didn't seem as if the night was ending anytime soon, and the Phoenix people were all in great spirits. The behavior bar in their town wasn't moving, and nothing that Alford had seen indicated that it would. He knew he needed to get back to his own town and began his goodbyes.

Saying goodbye to Bo was harder than he thought it would be. They hugged, and Alford got back into his car, ready for the long trip ahead. He was excited to see his family. As soon as the door shut and the engine turned over, his cell phone rang. It was an all-too-familiar tone.

"Yes sir," he answered.

"Honey, it's me," Beth said on the other line.

Alford was dumbfounded. Why was his wife on Grayson's phone? Why was Grayson at Alpha? His stomach did summersaults. Had his town been ReSet? He felt as if he was going to be sick.

"Beth?" He managed to mutter. "What is Grayson doing—" He couldn't finish before she interrupted.

"There's no time. This is serious," she said. He could hear the fear in her voice, which made him even sicker to his stomach. "Grayson has already sent a chopper. It'll be there in about ten minutes. We're sending coordinates to an open field near Phoenix. Get there now!"

she instructed. "David is calling Bo, so he can warn the city in case they hear the chopper."

"I don't understand," Alford replied as he felt the phone vibrate—no doubt the coordinates his wife had just promised. "What's wrong with Utopian?" he asked.

"It's not Utopian," she said. There was a pause on the line. Alford looked at his phone, sure he had lost the signal. Yet, there were four tiny dark bars at the top of the screen. "Beth!" he said, in an urgent voice. He could hear her whimpering now.

"Please, just get here," she begged. "It's Charlie."

THE HEART OF THE MATTER

The line went silent for what seemed like an eternity.

"Al, did you hear me?" Beth said. "It's Char. Please just get here."

He replayed what she had said in his head a couple of times. Panic and fear spread across his body like a wildfire.

"What happened?" He managed to say. "Is he okay?"

"There isn't time dear," Beth replied, her voice full of emotion. "They're calling for me. I have to go. Please just get to the chopper and get here as fast as you can."

She didn't even wait for a reply or say that she loved him. She hadn't done that since they almost divorced nearly a decade ago. They had made it a rule. After everything they had been through and everything they had seen, they knew one very important thing: life was precious, and you never knew when you would take your last breath. Because of this, they had made it a point to never hang up without saying "I love you". The fact that she had forgotten to say it amplified his fear.

He pushed the gas pedal harder, pulled the coordinates up from his text, and tried to focus on getting to the location safely. Grayson hadn't had to send a chopper for anything medical yet, so he knew this was something serious. Secretly, he knew it was probably life-threatening, but he wasn't allowing his mind to go there. He finally arrived at the location that was pre-determined for him. It was a large empty field surrounded by massive oak trees. Each tree looked as if it was preparing to give a performance as they stood tall with hundreds of large branches protruding from them. He was surprised to see that there was already another vehicle at the site facing him, its headlights disoriented him momentarily. Two dark figures got out of the vehicle and began approaching him, which would have normally made him uneasy, but all he could think about right now was Charlie. He killed his own engine and headed to meet the unknown figures. The trees' grandeur was doing an excellent job of covering the moonlight, so the entire field was nearly pitch black. Between that and the blinding headlights, even with his hands cupped around his eyes, Alford couldn't tell who he was walking toward.

"Over here, partner. You made good time," one of the voices hollered to him.

He recognized the voice immediately. They had just shared some special moments together. What he didn't know was what he was doing there.

"Bo," he began. "Why are you here?"

"I got a call right as you did, buddy," he said. "Grayson told me all about it. So, me and Jonas here, got in the car to meet you. Jonas has offered to take your car back to Utopian, and I'm here to bring Jonas and to show you my support."

Alford felt sick. If Grayson was making phone calls as well, this could be even worse than he'd imagined. He thanked both men for showing up. He extended his hand to Jonas, who shook it firmly, but there was a sadness in his eyes. Alford could tell that both of these men probably knew exactly what was going on. He was getting a little annoyed that somebody wouldn't fill him in as well.

Jonas Tankerson was to Bo what Sheriff Tate was to him. However, Bo had been afraid the idea of a "cop" and "cop shop" in the town might put the people on edge. So, he'd convinced Grayson that they would just have PI services. Bo had guessed the biggest crime that would happen in the new cities were people losing things—that there wouldn't be any crime at all. He wanted the idea of a person in town who had that law enforcement feel without an actual law enforcement presence. He thought this was the lowkey way to present it. Jonas had been a detective in his formal life. He worked child assault cases. He had seen the worst things possible and captured some of the most heinous perpetrators. Offering him this new position was like offering him retirement, and he was thrilled. He had said that after all the things he had seen and dealt with, a life of no crime and easy detective work was like a dream come true. He had a wife and one child, who was a few months younger than Charlie. In the beginning, Jonas had been hesitant to have children after everything that he'd seen, but deep down, he had always wanted a son. He was surprised when he came home that cold February morning after a very bad call and his wife had cooked. It was 3 a.m., and she should have been sleeping. Not only was it strange that she had cooked at the time she did, but she made pickles and pancakes. He threw his hands in the air and accused her of going mad. She simply smiled, got up from her seat, went to him, kissed him on the cheek, and said words he would never forget: "The baby gets what the baby wants; I'm not steering this ship." She cupped one hand below and one hand above her belly and just stood there. It took him a couple of seconds to grasp what she was saying, but when he did, a flood of emotions hit him all at once. He dropped to his knees and began kissing her belly. Nine months later, he got his baby boy, Tommy, and he vowed to protect him from the sick world they lived in, no matter the cost. Signing up with Grayson Jeffers, in a way, was doing just that.

He extended his hand to Bo as well, who pushed it away and wrapped him up in another Bo Bear Hug. He was caught off guard by how much he needed it. He broke free and locked eyes with Bo.

"Please, tell me what's going on," he said.

Bo looked at Jonas, who shrugged his shoulders. He looked back at Alford and paused.

"I can't," he said. "It's not my place, and I've been instructed by Grayson not to."

Alford could feel his anger boiling. Grayson had no right to make him wait. There was something big happening, with his child, and he needed to know, now.

"Bo, it's my son," he began. "Please, just tell me what is going on. You know Charlie. Please don't make me wonder. It's killing me."

Bo just stood there for a moment. He loved the Newsome family. They had been so good to him, and Alford had been like a big brother. He knew there was a chance Grayson was watching, though, and he also knew that he needed to keep orders in front of Jonas. He put his hands in his pockets and looked down. He couldn't do it.

Alford was in disbelief. How could Bo keep this from him? "Look at me, Bo," he said. Bo never moved. "Look at me!" he screamed.

Jonas and Bo weren't prepared for that. Nobody had ever heard Alford scream. Alford had even surprised himself. His tantrum had gotten both their attention, though, and he wasn't going to lose the momentum now.

"Bo, this is my son. How fair is it that you all know what's going on with him, and I'm left in the dark?" he said, his voice still elevated. The darkness of night was hiding his features, but Alford was sure they could hear the tears in his voice.

"I can't. It's Grayson," Bo said.

"I DON'T CARE IF IT IS THE POPE!" Alford yelled. "THIS IS MY SON. Tell me now, and I will deal with Grayson. He'll just have to understand."

Alford took a step closer to Bo and leaned in until he was almost nose to nose with him.

"Do you hear me, G.J.?" he asked. "You got an issue with Bo telling me, then you and I will deal with that at Alpha. These men have nothing to do with it. You should have kept them out of it.

So, Bo is going to tell me now, and you are going to be completely understanding of it. I appreciate it very much."

Alford stepped back and smiled at Bo, still unsure if he would see the gesture. He was trying his best to not appear manic.

"See Bo," he said. "It's handled. Now, will you please, for the love of everything, tell me what happened to my son!"

Bo shook his head. "I'm sorry I even hesitated to tell you a thing buddy. You know I'm in a tough position because we're dealing with Grayson, man. If you think that sweet talking you just did there will keep me outta trouble, I'll go ahead and tell you all that I know, but it ain't much."

Alford leaned against Bo's truck. He wasn't feeling well. "That's fine. I'll take what I can get at this point."

Bo opened his mouth to speak, and the sound of the medic chopper drowned him out. All three men looked in unison as the chopper was making its descent. Bo grabbed his hat before it flew off. The men took a step back as the chopper landed. Alford looked at Bo and decided not to waste any more time. He threw his keys to Jonas, who caught them midair. Then, he waved to them and ran toward the chopper.

As he got closer, the side door slid open. The sound of the grinding heavy metal competed against the blades of the chopper and won; it was deafening. He wondered who he would be flying with. He had hoped it wasn't Grayson; he wasn't sure he could control himself around him in his present emotional state. The passenger stuck his arm out to assist Alford in getting in and much to his surprise, it was David. Alford got in, and David slapped the window behind the pilot and slid the door shut as the chopper began to lift off the ground. Alford was dumbfounded; David was supposed to be kicking off a new city, too. What was he doing here? He stared out the tiny window as both Jonas and Bo got smaller. He saw Jonas getting into his car and driving off. He followed his car down the dark road until it became the size of a firefly. He imagined that his car was just that and he was anywhere but in the back of a cold medic chopper zooming off to a situation he still had no insight into. He pictured a warm summer breeze, a cold iced tea with more sugar than tea—just the way his mother had made it—and catching fireflies. He thought about this until he could no longer see the glow of the headlights. He knew the trip to Alpha would take less than an hour. He felt his arm being nudged and turned his head to see David extending headphones. He grabbed them and put them on.

"Al, I've been instructed to bring you to Alpha," David began.

"I don't care what Grayson has said to you," Alford interrupted. "Tell me what's going on!"

David bit his lip. Alford was not in the mood.

"David, I don't know what's been going on with you, but I'm sick of it. We aren't in a city right now. There are no behavior bars, and there is no threat of 'being bad', so, if you don't tell me what I want to know about Char, I swear I will grab you by your feet and hang you out of this chopper."

Alford watched as his friend's eyes widened with fear. He instantly felt guilty for acting that way, but these people had left him no choice.

"It's his heart," David blurted out. He didn't speak for a few more seconds. He was hoping he wouldn't have to say anything else. He was hoping that as long as Alford accepted just that, Grayson wouldn't be upset with him. He stared at Alford and knew it wasn't enough, though. He knew he would have to tell him everything. He took a deep breath and filled him in on what he knew.

He explained that he had just wrapped up his ceremony for the key city and they were going to have a "Chili Cook-Off and Dessert Contest" to get the community involved and to keep the spirits high. They had invited him to be the guest judge when his phone rang. Grayson had told him there was already a chopper waiting and that he had to go get Alford now. He was told that Charlie was in the field flying kites with Katie, while Beth was at the market picking up some things for dinner. They weren't sure exactly what happened.

They'd gone through the feed at least ten times to try to find out. One minute, the kids were laughing and playing; the next minute, Charlie was looking down the hill and not moving. Katie asked him twice what was wrong, and the next thing you know, he was on the ground, and everything went dark on Charlie's feed. Katie's feed was compromised because it was blurry because she was crying, but they could hear her screaming, "Help! Please someone help!" It was a miracle, though, because Sheriff Tate was in the area and heard little Katie and came to help. He was the one who called in a medical code and requested the chopper.

"Why did he need the chopper, Dave?" Alford asked.

David didn't answer immediately. He put his hand on Alford's and squeezed, his own eyes filling with tears.

"He was dead, Al," he managed to utter.

"Dead? What do you mean dead?" Alford asked.

"His heart wasn't registering on the monitors at Alpha, and the sheriff said he had no pulse when he got to him. He started CPR and was able to get him back right before the chopper got there, but Charlie's heart kept stopping all the way to Alpha. Last I heard, they were possibly going to operate, but Beth was arguing with them that they couldn't."

Alford slumped back in his seat. It didn't make any sense. His chip wasn't supposed to cause any issues unless under extreme physical exhaustion or high stress. Flying kites with his kid sister didn't meet either of those criteria. He grabbed his phone. He needed to talk to Beth. He felt like an idiot for not thinking of it sooner. She could give him more details. But it went straight to voicemail. He sighed. What happened?

They rode the rest of the way in silence. Alford checked his watch at least a dozen times. Each time, he was sure twenty minutes had elapsed. It seemed as if they were never going to make it.

"We're here," David said.

Alford looked out the window and didn't see anything at all. It was pitch black. He looked back at David in confusion.

"Oh, right. You haven't been here in a while," he said.

He unclipped a walkie-talkie from his shirt and pushed the button on the side. "Team Alpha, this is Chair #2 DK9722. We're at entry point three and approaching quickly with Medi3, please allow for entry. Over."

Alford was baffled. He had no idea what was going on.

"DK9722, you are clear for entry. Hover on standby while we unveil and then enter at will. Over" a husky voice replied back.

Alford heard a loud sound of grinding gears that made the chopper seem as if it was whispering. He put his hands over his ears, trying to muffle the sound. "What is that?" he mouthed to David, who mouthed back to look out the window. As Alford did, he was completely surprised by the new security measure that Grayson had taken. It appeared as if an iron curtain had been stretched out above Alpha, forming a dome. It was split into approximately fifteen layers that integrated as it opened. When the last layer joined the stack, the entire device tilted vertically and slide into the ground, as if it was never there. The chopper entered the medical bay. Alford was impressed and dumbfounded at the same time. There was no threat left in the United States; what was Grayson so afraid of?

"Pretty neat, huh?" David said. "We're completely off the grid and secure. Nobody is getting in here."

"Or out of here," Alford muttered under his breath. He didn't even wait to say anything else to David, instead breaking into a dead sprint toward the service elevator. He scanned his eyes, and the elevator kicked on. He got inside and pressed a button for the basement. David barely slid in to ride with him. It only was a few seconds later that the elevator door dinged. Alford was back in a full sprint. He ran down a long corridor that was only dimly lit. He began screaming.

"Beth, I'm here." He screamed. "Beth!"

She stepped out of the waiting room, her eyes stained with makeup. No doubt she had spent a lot of time crying. He ran to meet her, and they embraced. She hugged him so tightly, it made him fear the worst. He tried to let go, but she wouldn't let him. She began sobbing into his chest. He got a sick feeling in his gut and began to sob too. He heard whispers behind him. He recognized both voices and knew it was David and Grayson. He felt the anger fill his belly. He heard Grayson say, "No" in a hushed voice, and he lost it. He forced his wife away by her shoulders and held her face. Her sobs got even louder. He didn't want to hear her response, but he had to know.

"Where's Charlie?" he asked. She lifted her hand and pointed to an exam room across the hall. The lights were off, and there was nobody in there. He turned to look back at his dear wife and feared her response.

"Is he ... Is he," he stammered. "Is he dead?"

HEARTBEAT OF TRUTH

Beth was taken aback by her husband's question. She wasn't processing everything like she normally did, and it hadn't even crossed her mind that her husband was completely in the dark about what was going on. She grabbed Alford by the hand and squeezed tightly. "No, thank God, but he's barely alive. Go. Go see him."

Alford didn't hesitate and began across the hall to the exam room. He could hear his wife's faint footsteps behind him. He looked up above the door as he entered. Exam Room 4. A cold chill ran down his spine. This was the exact room that he was in when they had the chip mishap all those years ago. He wondered if sheer irony put his son in this room or if Grayson was playing a sick game with his mind. He felt anger deep in the pit of his stomach. He had to ignore it because right now his son needed his full attention. He would deal with Grayson later.

He threw the door open, and the sight of his son hit him like a ton of bricks. He had a tube running into his mouth, and his head was wrapped in white gauze. There was only a small table lamp on, and the faint glow of the light somehow made the situation even grimmer. His son was average size, but it seemed as if the hospital bed swallowed him whole. He was dressed in a tattered hospital gown with navy blue checks. All elements that made Charlie who he was had been stripped away, and only a shell remained. He felt the warm tears running down his face. He walked slowly to him as if his footsteps would wake him, but he knew that his son wasn't conscious. He sat in the chair that his wife had surely been occupying, leaned over on his son's body, and broke down. He began apologizing repeatedly until he felt a hand rubbing his back.

"This isn't your fault," his wife said quietly. "There's nothing you could have done."

"I need to know what happened," Alford said. "I got the intro from David, but I need to know what happened after the sheriff called it in."

His wife shook her head. She was more than willing to fill him in, although she was still dumbfounded as well. "Some of it's very confusing to me, and hopefully when you meet with Dr. Heathrow, he can answer the more technical questions that you have," she said. "Dr. Heathrow had gone with the chopper and took over for Sheriff Tate as soon as they landed in Utopian. The sheriff stayed back to monitor the city and keep things running. Dr. Heathrow hooked Charlie up to several monitors in the chopper and kept getting bizarre readings on the monitor. Charlie's heart wasn't beating normally and would randomly stop. He said the very first readings were also strange because it appeared as if Charlie's heart originally stopped due to fear or a panic attack so strong it messed with his heart rhythms—and due to how sensitive it was, it killed him."

"If the sheriff hadn't been there and resituated at the exact moment he did, Charlie wouldn't be lying in that bed. Once back at Alpha, his team joined him and they had to open Charlie's chest, but he said he knew he couldn't use the same anesthesia as they had before because of how stressful it was on Charlie's heart. He gave him a mild sedative, and he slowly administered three different doses of medicine until he had him in a fully-induced coma and on a machine to breathe, alleviating as much of the pressure that his body was under as possible, trying to give him a better chance to recover from whatever was going on. He said it was a risk and something he had never done before, but the alternative was doing nothing."

"They had to open his chest and they found out that Charlie's heart had dead scar tissue leftover from his frequent heart issues. There was evidence that some of his heart episodes were worse than maybe even Charlie realized, and he was having mini heart attacks. His heart isn't functioning the way it should."

Alford was trying to process everything as rapidly as his wife was saying it to him. She was right, though. There were still so many unanswered questions.

"Where is Dr. Heathrow now?" Alford asked.

"Meeting with Grayson in his office," she replied.

He stood up, kissed his wife on the forehead, and headed out to find the good doctor.

She took his place in the chair and began pushing back Charlie's hair from his head.

"Where is Katie?" he asked before exiting.

"She's with Mick and Sal back at Utopian," she answered. "I wasn't sure what we would be dealing with here and didn't want to expose her, in case ... well, if it was the worst-case scenario."

He smiled faintly at his wife. He wanted to be stronger for her, but the last couple of hours had completely drained him emotionally. He left the exam room and headed back down the corridor. Then, he scanned his eyes and headed up the service elevator to the top floor. The doors opened with a ding, and he stepped inside. It had been years since he had been back, and everything here still looked the same. This top level of Alpha was Grayson's personal space. He lived and worked here. The entire upper level was carpeted in deep-red velvet. The walls were embossed and painted in gold. All the furniture was as black as the night. It had a Hollywood Glamour feel to it, which was so weird given Grayson's rugged and macho exterior. You would have expected to see camouflage carpet and animal carcasses all over the walls with handmade furniture—compliments of the very trees that stood outside Alpha. Only the chairmen had access to the top floor, but each one of them was as shocked as the next when they stepped off the elevator and into this area. It didn't seem like a place Grayson Jeffers belonged. He had once joked to Al that he wanted the carpet blood red in case things ever got out of hand with anyone, you wouldn't be able to tell. Alford had slightly chuckled at the time, but after almost ten years with Grayson, he was afraid it wasn't a joke.

Right off the elevator was a reception desk where Grayson's assistant of twenty years worked. Her name was DeeDee. Although you could tell she was past her youthful years and appeared to be the neighborhood grandmother because of her wrinkled face, frizzy ash-gray hair—always pulled back in a tight bun—and sensible shoes, she was fierce and didn't put up with nonsense from anybody. She was the only person who could call Grayson out in front of people and live to joke about it. Grayson never shared many sentiments, but you could tell he loved DeeDee. He had a soft spot for her and you could tell that he had subconsciously put her in a motherly role. He had even proved his love by allowing her to bring her cat Annabelle to Alpha, and he was allergic to cats. His allergies were so bad that they would ruin his whole day. He took a daily allergy shot just so he could work around DeeDee. Even though she didn't bring Annabelle to the top floor, she always had her cat hair on her clothing and personal items. This was proof to everyone who knew them that DeeDee was special to Grayson. No doubt, he could depend on her. Truth be told, all of Alpha depended on her. Beyond her desk in the center of the room was Grayson's conference area. He had enclosed the entire conference space in bullet and soundproof glass. You could see into it, but you couldn't hear anything. It looked more like a prison than a meeting area. There was a long black table with marble legs and ten high-back dark leather chairs with gold studs adorning the legs pulled underneath it. He could see Grayson and Dr. Heathrow discussing something. There was a file open on the table. On the other side of the conference table were three doors. The center door was always locked, and only two people had access,

Grayson and DeeDee. These were Grayson's sleeping quarters and kitchen space. He also kept a safe with things in it that nobody knew about it. The door to the left opened to the master computer mainframe. The chairs, DeeDee, and Grayson had access to that room, and it was where all the data collected from the cities was stored. The door to the right was Grayson's idea room. It was basically his office, but he said he didn't go there to work; he went there to innovate. It had his personal laptop, a small desk, and five filing cabinets in it. There was one for Alpha, and one for each key city. They contained the files on every person who survived the ReSet. The chairs, DeeDee, and Grayson had access to that room as well.

"I'm sorry, Mr. Newsome," DeeDee said. "You can't go in there. Mr. Jeffers is meeting with Dr. Heathrow, and you aren't on the list to enter the meeting."

Alford stopped dead in his tracks. She couldn't be serious. He knew they were meeting about his son.

"DeeDee," he began. "You know as well as I do that they're meeting about Charlie. You also know that there's something very wrong going on with him, and I need answers."

Her eyes were sad. She too loved Charlie. Charlie had done a great job of being someone that everyone loved and admired. He had been a special kid growing up at Alpha, and although his parents didn't know it, everyone frequently tuned in to watch Charlie on the feed as he was continuing his adventure in Utopian. They were all amazed at how good he was. He was the best brother, son, and friend that they had ever seen. He was better than all the adults, and they were just in awe. He had a great family, which no doubt contributed to how great he was, but even his sister had marks on the bar, and she was a pretty special kid as well. He hadn't gotten any. He was a child and had managed to behave better than an entire town.

"Look," she said. "I'm sorry, and I understand you want answers. We all do. However, you know that I answer to Grayson and Grayson only, and his orders were to not allow anyone into this meeting. So,

I am going to have to ask you to go back down to the med bay, and someone will be down to speak with you as soon as they can." She pushed a button under her desk and the elevator opened with a ding that made Alford jump.

"DeeDee," he said calmly. "I have known you half the time you have known Grayson. I love you—I truly do—and you have been great to my family. I mean this as respectfully as I can, but nothing you say or do is going to get me on that elevator. I am not leaving here until I speak with one or both of those men. Now, if you don't mind, I will speak to Grayson about it, and you know he won't be mad at you for a thing."

Satisfied she understood where he was coming from, he took a step forward toward the conference room, both men's backs now to him. He took a few more steps and heard a sickening sound. He wasn't sure he had heard it correctly until DeeDee's question confirmed it.

"Now, Mr. Newsome, please tell me you aren't going to make me shoot you?"

He slowly turned around, hoping that what he had just heard wasn't true. But it was. As he fully turned around, he saw that sweet Ms. DeeDee had pulled out a shotgun from ... somewhere and was aiming it right at him, her eyes locked on to him and her finger on the trigger.

"What are you doing, you crazy lady?" Alford asked in fear. He couldn't believe this. His son was fighting for his life, and Grayson's assistant was pulling a gun on him just because he wanted to talk.

"I told you that Mr. Jeffers was unavailable right now. So, if you would kindly make your way to the elevator, he will be with you when he can," she said.

Alford slowly began walking toward the elevator. No wonder Grayson kept her around. He knew she was tough, but this was next-level. He was inches from the elevator, and he heard her chuckle.

"That's a good choice," she said. "Now, I will be happy to tell Mr. Jeffers you stopped by. We'll be praying for little Charlie. Bless his heart."

Alford still couldn't believe she was forcing him to leave at gunpoint. He got into the elevator, scanned his eyes, and pushed the basement button to head down to the med bay. He was making a mental list of all the things he planned on discussing with Grayson. He was two floors from the basement when the elevator jolted, stopped, and then began climbing back up. He hadn't touched anything and was confused about what was happening. The doors opened, and he hid behind them for a minute, afraid of DeeDee. He slowly peeked around the corner to see her typing away at her computer.

He stepped off the elevator and cleared his throat.

"Oh, lovely to see you, Mr. Newsome. We're so sorry to hear about Charlie. Me and Annabelle are saying extra special prayers. Mr. Jeffers has requested to see you. You may join him and Dr. Heathrow in the conference room," she said.

Alford just stared at her and blinked repeatedly. How was this the same woman who was prepared to shoot him dead just moments before? Was she psychotic? He managed a forced smile and headed to the conference room. He entered, and Grayson motioned for him to sit down.

"Good to see you, Mr. Newsome," Grayson said. "Sorry it was under these circumstances. However, I want to start with a few things. If you ever tell one of my people to defy a direct order again, you will be the one on an exam table. Do you understand me?"

Alford looked coldly at Grayson. He had so much he wanted to say, but now was not the time. He needed information about his son. So, he bit his tongue, swallowed his pride, and nodded.

"Yes, sir," he said dryly. "It was a very tense time, and I was not acting like myself because of the situation with my son. I was desperate for answers."

"Which is the only reason I am not making a big deal of it," Grayson replied. "Dr. Heathrow will fill you in on what we know. I'm going to call Mr. Billings to remind him that when I give a direct order, it stands, and nobody overrules it. For now, it will be a warning. You gentlemen can stay in here, and when you're finished, DeeDee will see you out." He pushed his chair back and exited the conference room.

As soon as he left, the tension eased from the room. Alford got up and shook Dr. Heathrow's hand.

"It is really good to see you, Paul," Alford said. "Please, tell me what's going on."

Paul hesitated at first. Alford could tell something was going on. He opened his mouth to speak and closed it again. "Look, I don't know how to say this," he said. "I once again don't have very good news about Charlie. I still don't know what happened that started this, but I do know more now about what's been going on for the last six to seven years. His heart isn't keeping up. The frequent monitoring of the chip is giving Charlie mini heart attacks and killing off areas of his heart. Eventually, there won't be enough good muscle left, and his heart will give out."

"Well, can we take the chip out?" Alford asked.

"Afraid not," Dr. Heathrow said. "We can't do an X-Ray because it could possibly interfere with the chip and could damage him more. We can't remove his entire heart. Grayson wanted me to put another chip in his leg or somewhere else, but the two chips would cancel each other out as far as monitoring is concerned."

"I don't care about the stupid monitoring," Alford said.

"I know, but Grayson does," Dr. Heathrow answered. "Right now, Charlie's feed is going to forever be scattered. Basically, it will be hit and miss, and we will only get bits and pieces of it. Grayson is forming a specific "Charlie" team whose jobs are going to be unscrambling the bits and pieces of recordings and trying to create daily timelines. Imagine that every heartbeat is giving a snapshot of what he is doing and saying, so you have pictures, but some of it will have gaps. So, they'll put together as much as they can, but there will be things missing in between. For now, we need to let Charlie's heart rest for about a week before we pull him off the machines. Every day will be a guess on if his heart makes it. We need to watch him even more now than we did before. I'm so sorry this is happening. Your family—especially Charlie—doesn't deserve this. I have done everything I can."

"I thank you for that. You saved my boy once, and I know I won't be able to repay you," Alford said. "I must get back to him. Thank you again." Alford got up from the table and headed to the door. Dr. Heathrow sat there, sick to his stomach. There was one more piece of information he wanted to tell him, something he had wanted to tell him for a very long time now, but he knew that he never really would be able to—not without betraying Grayson and suffering the ramifications that would cause.

Alford had made it to the door and was seconds from leaving. "You know," he said. "I have thanked you so many times for saving Charlie all those years ago, but I've never asked you to forgive me."

Dr. Heathrow sat speechlessly. He had no idea what Alford would need forgiveness for.

"Forgive you," he asked. "For what?"

"For being so angry at you," Alford said. "I was so angry about the chip mistake, but accidents happen, and I had absolutely no right to be angry at you. I'm sorry."

Dr. Heathrow stared at Alford. Here was a man who had lost so much in life, and now his boy, his special son, was fighting for his life, and he was taking the time to apologize for something tragic that had happened when he had no idea what the truth entailed. He had no idea it hadn't been an accident at all. The very reason Charlie was in this position today was because of something Grayson had done, against Dr. Heathrow's advice—something that was unnecessary—and this man who had served him faithfully had no idea. Dr. Heathrow couldn't stand it any longer.

"Alford," he said. "Sit down, we need to talk."

SECRETS REVEALED

Alford stopped. He wasn't sure what else there was to explain, and he was desperate to see his son.

"Is this important, Paul?" he asked. "I really need to head back to Charlie."

"It is," Paul replied. "If you don't mind shutting the door ... what I'm going to say can't leave this room."

Paul looked over his shoulder and noticed DeeDee was staring at them over her glasses, momentarily stopping whatever it was she had been working on. Alford turned slowly to stare at Paul. He could tell immediately by the look on his face that something was terribly wrong. He knew this had to be really bad to stop him from seeing his son when he needed his father the most. He slowly walked over to the table and placed his hands on the back of the black chair.

"You probably need to sit down," Paul said.

Alford shook his head, confused. "Just say it, Paul. I'm fine to stand, and I can handle whatever it is that you need to tell me."

"Please, will you just sit down? DeeDee is already suspicious, and nobody can know what I'm about to say. So, please just sit, and try to look normal."

Paul looked over his shoulder again. DeeDee had returned to her busywork but was still eyeing the conference room. Alford met his gaze and picked up instantly on DeeDee's suspicious look. He walked over to Paul, patted him on the back, shook his head, and sat down. He was trying to appear as if everything was fine, even though in the pit of his stomach he didn't think he was prepared to hear what Paul had to say. Paul looked back over his shoulder and opened the file that was in front of him. He waited a second, and DeeDee seemed satisfied. She smiled and looked back at her desk to continue her work.

Paul took a deep breath and turned back to face Alford. He knew what he was about to say would be risky; he was worried this wasn't the right choice. He was still so grieved by Alford's sincere apology. He had sworn he would take Grayson's secret to the grave, mainly because he was afraid if he didn't, Grayson would be making sure that grave was personally dug himself. He could feel the sweat beginning to bead around the temples of his head. He wiped it with the back of his hand and sat back in his chair. He had made a big mistake. He couldn't tell Alford. He had no idea what would happen to himself, to the Newsome family, and to Utopian. He had to come up with a lie; he had to find a way to get Alford out of this room.

"Actually, Al," he began. "We can talk later. Let's go check on Charlie together." He forced a smile but could now feel the sweat dripping down the side of his face. He lifted the front of his shirt and wiped it away.

"Paul," Alford said calmly. "I'm not sure what's going on here. I'm not sure what you have to tell me, but I do know that you are one of the best people I have ever met. I have appreciated your honesty throughout the years while you have helped with Charlie. Even when we didn't want to hear what you had to say, you didn't sugarcoat it. You have helped us more than you can possibly know, and I want you to know we will do the same for you. Whatever is going on here, we are here for you. If you are in trouble, I want to help you. Please, let me repay you for saving Charlie then and now. It's the least I can do."

"It was Grayson," Paul blurted out. His eyes widened and he cupped his hands over his mouth, desperately wishing he could suck his words back from the air and swallow them. He couldn't believe he said it. Why was Alford such a good guy? He could tell by the look on Alford's face that he was going to have to give a detailed explanation, but for the moment, he felt like he could breathe a little easier getting that off his chest. He didn't wait for Alford to question him; he knew it was time.

"Grayson is the reason Charlie is in trouble today; the reason he will probably die young. I'll tell you everything," he said.

For the next thirty minutes, Paul explained to Alford everything that had happened almost ten years before. He could see the shock in Alford's face—followed by the disgust. He knew he was starting something that couldn't be stopped, but he felt the need to continue. He should have softened some of the details, but he didn't. He told the cold, hard truth. He could see the horror on his face when he spoke about Grayson being the one to do the injection. He didn't know what to say to rectify the situation. There was silence between the two men after the secret was revealed. The only sound you could hear was the steady tapping of Alford's fingers on the conference table. Alford was staring in the distance, and if it weren't for the rhythmic tapping, you could question if he was even alive. It was starting to make Paul uncomfortable.

"I don't know what to say," he began.

"Please, just don't say anything," Alford replied. "This whole time, I thought you saved my son. This whole time I thought this was an unavoidable situation that happened. If I understood correctly, this didn't have to happen at all. We could have skipped the monitoring of Charlie and he may have never had a heart condition. He wouldn't be lying in that bed, hooked to tubes, fighting for his life. He would have a chance at a normal, long, healthy life," he shouted as he slammed his hand on the table.

Paul was glad DeeDee couldn't hear inside this room, and he was glad that their monitoring chips were shut off the minute they entered Grayson's executive suite. "The damage was already done, and he swore me to secrecy; I didn't think I really had a choice in this matter."

Alford held his hand up to stop Paul from speaking. "I'm not angry with you," he said.

His tone had suddenly changed and was eerily calm. His eyes dilated and his expression had changed too. The ever-friendly Mr. Newsome now looked like a stone-cold killer. In that moment, Paul regretted saying anything at all. Alford stood from his chair, tucked it in, extended his hand, and smiled. Paul slowly lifted his hand to meet Al's. They exchanged a firm handshake, and Alford began to exit the room.

Paul was confused and worried. "What, what, are you going to do, Alford?" Paul asked. "What are you going to say?" Paul knew his life was over. He stared patiently at Alford, who once again was standing at the door with his back to him. He wished he could go back to the moment before he left the room and simply say you're welcome. Alford looked back over his shoulder at Paul and smiled. That alarmed Paul more than anything. This smile was devious and made him feel like he, too, was in danger.

"Nothing," Alford said calmly. Paul sighed with relief. He knew Alford was a good man. He had already found it in his heart to forgive Grayson. He also stood up and closed his file, ready to leave the tension-filled room.

"Nothing, for now," Alford added as he left.

Paul could hear the coldness in his voice. Alford was done with Grayson; he knew it in that moment. Now Paul was stuck between two worlds. Should he warn Grayson what he had done and risk immediate death? Should he trust that Alford would leave his name out of things? He knew Alford couldn't take on Grayson Jeffers, the top dog of Alpha. He was the very reason they were all still alive. Al would be foolish. It would be a suicide mission. He had no idea what was going to happen in the coming days. He watched as Alford easily walked past DeeDee, flashed her a smile, and got on the elevator. As the doors shut, he saw his face go dark again. Had he just created a monster?

As the elevator doors shut, Alford broke down in tears. He couldn't believe what he had just heard. How could somebody he had devoted his life to—someone whose cause he had championed—do something so terrible to his child? Grayson Jeffers was more than just trying to set the world right; he was trying to play God. He quickly remembered that they monitored the elevators and knew he needed an explanation for his emotional outburst. The last thing that he needed to happen was Grayson to be standing on the other side of the doors. He wasn't ready to see him.

He dropped to his knees and cried out, "Charlie, I should have been there." He expressed real emotion because a big part of him regretted ever leaving his family. Satisfied this would answer any concerns the monitoring team would have, he let himself cry a few more moments and stood up to compose himself. He stepped off the elevator door and made his way back down the med bay hallway. This time, he was slow in his steps. He needed a moment to clear his head. For now, he had no intention of reacting to what he had found out, and he knew better than to tell Beth. Years ago, he had to convince her that everything was still on track and that they had made the right choice siding with Grayson. He would eventually tell her what had happened, but this was not the time and certainly not the place. He made it back to the exam room to find that his wife had fallen asleep holding Charlie's hand. He stood in the doorway and just stared at his family. He wished Katie was with them so they could all be together. He decided he didn't want to wake Beth just yet. He wanted a few more moments to decompress. He also wanted to check in on Utopian. He made his way to the tiny waiting room, praying somebody had made a pot of coffee. He realized it had almost been twenty-four hours, and he had yet to sleep. As he entered the waiting room, he noticed the black and white checkered tile. It was hideous. There were cobwebs in each corner of the room, and the trash can was spilling over. There were four maroon waiting room chairs pushed up against a window. Each cushion had been ripped and worn down. He had never paid much attention to this place because every time that he was there, he was always preoccupied with the bad news he was receiving, but he wondered if it was always in such bad shape. He couldn't imagine that it had been because Grayson had expensive taste. Everything that Grayson had to build his empire he collected from destroyed cities, but it would be out of character for him to pick something so dilapidated. He thought of the countless people who had sat in those chairs waiting for their loved ones to be implanted. He assumed that this explained the condition of the chairs. He thought of the relief that everyone had when Dr. Heathrow entered, a smile on his face, with good news in tow. His family had been the only one that didn't receive good news. He could feel his temper rising and knew he needed a distraction. He fished his phone out of his pocket and pressed hard on the number four.

Within one ring, a man on the other line answered. "What do we know? How is Char? How is Beth? Heck, how are you?" the man rapidly asked, giving Alford no time to respond.

"Slow down, Dave," Alford responded. "We're okay for now, but I'm calling to check on Katie and Utopian. By now, I am sure you have made it back. I want Katie here and need to see if you can call Grayson to arrange that."

"Why would I call him?" David asked.

Alford paused a moment. He knew he couldn't tell David the real reason. He knew it could very well be the end for both of them. He couldn't tell him that if he saw Grayson right now, he was afraid he would try to rip his heart out so he could see what it felt like. He couldn't tell him that he was starting to be concerned that the whole plan was a mistake and that he felt he would need to step up and make things right. He couldn't tell him any of this because he wasn't sure he could trust him.

"Because," he began. "You're his second in command and can make that request on my behalf. I really need to be able to focus on Charlie and Beth, but I also want Katie here and I know I can trust you to do that." He was at least glad he still did trust that David King would never do anything to hurt Katie or Charlie. He was like their uncle.

"You bet I can," he said. "Even if I have to bring her in myself. How long are you going to be there? Grayson told me to prepare myself to handle things at Utopian for a bit. How long is a bit?"

Alford rolled his eyes but made sure to keep his voice level. "Dr. Heathrow says at least a week. They want to give Charlie a chance to allow his heart to rest before waking him up. We'll know more once they do that."

The men finished working out the details on getting Katie to Alpha, and David gave him a quick update on Utopian. The whole town was doing really well, and they hadn't received any marks over the last four days. They were trying hard to be extra good to make Alford proud and to honor Charlie. Kids from their school had made him cards, and the whole town was concerned. Alford thanked David for everything and got off the phone. He didn't want to speak too long because he was afraid he would let something slip that would reveal how he really felt.

After the call ended, Alford slouched into one of the waiting room chairs. He felt emotionally drained. He had no idea how he was going to do this with Beth. She would see right through him. He needed a better plan for her. His stomach growled, and he realized he was hungry. He walked over to the vending machine and pulled his wallet out. Empty. Just his luck. He looked around the room, and a genuine smile spread across his face. He wondered if it would still work. He tapped the left side of the machine three times and then kicked the bottom once. He waited for the whirling sound and then gave it one hard shake, and a bag of chips dropped to the bottom. He chuckled to himself.

"Good ole E7," he said out loud.

He tried to think back to when he realized this machine did this, and the cruel irony smacked him in the face yet once again. It was when he had just found out about the chip implant having gone wrong. He had gone to the waiting room to cool off and tried to get a snack cake. It wouldn't work, and after the machine had taken his three dollars, he slapped the machine three times. Unfortunately, this just caused his hand to hurt, so he got angrier and kicked the machine. Somehow in that process, he jammed his toe, and feeling like he couldn't take anything else, he shook the machine. As if to humble him, a bag of potato chips fell from the machine. He had tried this trick three other times after that, and it had worked all three times. He was grateful now for his snack, but the memory had brought him sadness again. He needed another distraction and remembered why he had walked in there in the first place. He walked across the room to the corner where the coffee station was.

Much to his surprise, there was a pot of coffee made. It was half gone, and no doubt not very fresh, but it was hot. He was particular about how he liked his coffee and looked in the cabinets and mini fridge below to get his ingredients. He needed this coffee to be the best cup he had ever made. He felt his sanity may very well depend on it. He found what he was looking for and began doctoring his cup of coffee. When it was finished, he cupped his hands around it. The warmth felt nice. The dark roast of the coffee beans filled his nostrils. He loved the smell of coffee. In that moment, he felt okay. He was so lost in his cup that he didn't even hear the approaching footsteps.

Suddenly, someone spoke from behind him. "Six Splenda and easy cream still how you take it, Newsome?"

He couldn't believe that this man had once again ruined a good moment. He hadn't even gotten a sip yet. He slowly placed the coffee cup down. He wasn't ready to face him. He needed more time. He didn't know how to control himself. He felt his fists clenching in front of him, his face getting hot with anger. He hoped that he would just walk away, but he knew better. He knew he would have to turn and face him, but he didn't know how.

"Did you hear me?"

Alford closed his eyes and inhaled sharply. He tried to think of everything that made him happy, but his mind kept going dark. He had no plan, but he had no choice. He turned slowly to face him. "Hello Grayson," he said.

CHARLIE HAS A SECRET TOO

I asked if you still take your coffee the same, Grayson replied. "I know you're going through some things, and it's been a while since you've been back here, but I'm accustomed to someone responding when I talk to them." He stared at Alford with ice blue eyes.

Usually, this made Alford uncomfortable, and he often felt the need to look away. The mix of the stark-white military cut and the cold eyes always made him feel like he couldn't look directly at him—like he may turn into stone if he did. This time, he felt different. This time, intimidation wasn't a factor, and without even realizing it, he was staring right back, challenging him. Grayson raised his eyebrows and took a step toward Alford. Alford realized that he had better react differently or Grayson would know that something was up. He quickly averted his eyes and looked back to his coffee cup. He needed to buy himself some time.

"Yes sir," he said as he grabbed his cup. "Just the same. A little coffee with my cream," he said, attempting a joke. Grayson didn't laugh, but Alford didn't expect him to. He took a large drink of his coffee, needing something to keep his mouth shut before he said what he really wanted to.

"That's better," Grayson said. "I trust you found out all you needed to from Dr. Heathrow."

Alford spit his coffee out all over the floor. “If you only knew,” he said, forgetting again that he needed to shut his mouth and keep it shut. He really needed sleep; he was not handling the situation very well. He turned to grab a few napkins to clean up the mess he had just made. He could feel Grayson’s glare beaming down on him.

“Newsome, what in the world has gotten into you?” Grayson said with disgust. “I know this is stressful for you and Beth, but you’ll get through it. We’re all here for you, and this will not be an excuse for such erratic behavior. You’re a chairperson; you need to get it together.”

Alford had already finished cleaning the droplets of coffee, but he was too angry to stand. How dare he say those things to him after what he’d done? He decided to continue his circular motions to appear as if he was still cleaning. If he stood now, his fist might end up connecting with Grayson’s mouth.

“Anyway,” Grayson started again. “I’ve set up quarters for your whole family here at Alpha while you wait for Charlie to heal. We’ll see how things are in a week. While you’re here, I look forward to sitting and chatting with you to check on things and see where your head is regarding the mission. Of course, I know you will need to prioritize that, and I don’t want to take away from what you feel you need to do with Charlie, so it’s not a meeting we need to have until tomorrow afternoon.”

Alford was dumbfounded. Grayson couldn’t be serious. Alford hadn’t showered or really gotten any sleep in almost an entire day. He hadn’t really spent any time with Charlie and now he was worried about a meeting about the mission. He felt the anger boiling again. He needed to speak up but was still concerned about looking him in the eye.

“Perhaps ... don’t you think even later in the week would be better suited for a mission meeting?” Alford said as he slowly stood to face Grayson.

Grayson’s ice blue eyes turned a dark gray, and he pursed his lips together. You could see his entire face turn dark red, even through his hair. “I thought I made myself clear,” he began. “I give orders and I expect them to be carried out. This is the last chance I can give you on this, and I’m only doing it because of the circumstances. I have been nothing but gracious to your family, and after everything I’ve done to help you, I can’t believe you have the audacity to question me. Remember your place, Newsome. You are what you are today because of me.”

Alford couldn’t take it. He was right. They were what and where they were today because of Grayson. His son was dying because of Grayson. In that moment, he forgot all about developing a plan. He wasn’t thinking about consequences, he was just seeing red. He opened his mouth to let Grayson have it and readied his fists. He took a step toward him and was interrupted.

“Oh, there you are, sweetie,” he heard his angelic wife say. “I’m sorry to interrupt, but Charlie is moving around, which he shouldn’t be doing, and I think you need to come quickly.”

He was grateful she showed up when she did because he’d just almost made a huge mistake.

He looked back at Grayson who looked confused and walked right past him. He pushed all his anger to the side and headed with his wife down the hall. He could hear Grayson following them.

“What was that all about?” his wife asked in a hushed voice.

“Nothing you need to worry about,” he said, grabbing her hand for reassurance.

They made it to Charlie’s room as Dr. Heathrow was checking him with a stethoscope. Charlie was moving his legs and making small, muffled noises.

“What’s happening?” Alford asked.

“I honestly don’t know,” Dr. Heathrow replied. “He shouldn’t be doing this. Some involuntary movement is possible while under sedation, but this is coherent and active movement. I think he’s trying to wake himself up, which shouldn’t be possible. The concoction of sedatives I created can’t be administered for another three hours. If I don’t do something, though, his heart could stop from the stress of trying to wake. I have no choice but to reintroduce a different kind of sedative, but I'm not sure how he will react to it. Yet, if we do nothing, he could have a massive heart attack."

Beth burst into tears. She wasn't strong enough to lose another child. Alford grabbed her in his arms and embraced her, tears staining his shirt.

"You have to make a decision as his parents," Dr. Heathrow said.

"I don't know, I just need a minute to think," Alford said. He wished he would have gotten that cup of coffee down.

"Just do it, Heathrow," Grayson said from the back of the room.

A violent chill ran down Alford's spine. He couldn't believe what he had just heard. This brazen man was trying to make a call about his son's health once again. At least this time he had the nerve to do it in front of him. Alford pushed Beth slowly back, cupped her face with his hands, and wiped her cheeks. He then turned to face Grayson; this time unafraid to back down.

"What right do you think you have to make a decision like that, now or ever?" Alford asked. "I'm his father, not you. We are the parents to whom Dr. Heathrow was speaking, not you. We make the life-altering decisions about his health, not you."

Grayson looked genuinely shocked that Alford challenged him yet again, and it pleased Alford.

"Alford," Grayson began. "I am truly afraid you have spent too many years at Utopian and have lost your way a little. You may be the big shot there, but please remember all that's left in this world is my pond, and I'm the big fish. I have given you freedom and have tried desperately to be very understanding during this time, but that was the final straw. That will be dealt with as I see fit tomorrow in our meeting. For now, I interjected because I can think logically. You don't have another choice. Doing nothing leaves a huge chance that he will have a heart attack. Isn't a small chance better than no chance?"

Alford opened his mouth and shut it again. Grayson was correct in his statement, and it made Alford livid. He didn't want him to have any validity in the things he was saying. While he was trying to separate his emotions from his decision, his son began to make noises again. All four people walked closer to him. It was as if Charlie was trying to communicate.

"Al, we have to do something," Beth said, tears still streaming down her face. She grabbed Charlie's hand. "We're here, baby. We're here."

Alford looked back to Dr. Heathrow who looked white as a ghost. No doubt, he was afraid that the truth he had revealed was about to come out in this small room and he had no escape from it. Dr. Heathrow put his hand on Alford's shoulder.

"Listen, I know what you're thinking right now—all of it," he said. He glanced back toward Grayson. "I know what you must be feeling, but none of that matters. Not right now. He's right. This is Charlie's only chance, and I'll be honest; it's a slim chance."

Alford grabbed Charlie's other hand and rubbed the back of it.

"Listen, Champ. You've gotta pull through. We need you to fight with everything you have. Katie will be here soon, and she needs to see you. We all need you to stay in this and not give up."

He felt his words getting caught in his throat, and he had to stop talking for a second. He leaned down to Charlie's ear and whispered one final thing.

"I can't do this without you, Champ. I love you ..." Then, turning, he said, "Do it, Paul."

***

A week had come and gone at Alpha and Charlie was pulling through. Katie had arrived and was distraught to see her brother in the state he was in. Luckily, David had gotten permission to leave Utopian in the hands of Sheriff Tate and come to help with Katie. This made for a good distraction for her. Alford did have his meeting with Grayson, and it didn't end well for Alford. He had convinced himself to sit in the room and not argue or say anything. Seeing his son survive the new sedative gave him the clarity he needed to know two things: he didn't think he could take down Grayson Jeffers alone, and he couldn't put his family at risk by acting so foolishly in the moment.

Alford's big punishment was that he had to do fifty training hours on subordinance and then he had to report daily to Sheriff Tate what he had done for the day. Essentially, Grayson had just officially made Sheriff Tate Al's boss, and he was not too keen on it. This only solidified his suspicions of Tate and now, sadly, David King. He didn't want to waste his time with things he couldn't control, though. He spent all of his free time with his family. It was finally time for Dr. Heathrow to try and bring Charlie back, and you could feel the nerves amongst everyone. Grayson insisted on also being in the room, and Katie wanted David there. Alford didn't feel like fighting, so he agreed.

Charlie's parents stood by his side, and everyone else stood toward the back of the room. Everyone held their breath as Dr. Heathrow began the tedious process of removing the tubes and unhooking the machines. Once he was done, he explained that it would be a waiting process. Ten minutes felt like ten hours, but Charlie began moving his hand. Katie saw it first and let out a delightful squeal.

Beth grabbed Charlie's hand and squeezed. "That's right, honey," she said sweetly. "It's okay. It's time to wake up."

Charlie then moved his left leg. At first, it was a twitching movement, but it morphed into a side-to-side motion. Dr. Heathrow explained that lying in bed for a week affected muscle memory, and his body was trying to figure out how to use its limbs again. After a few more moments, he tried to lift his head. Dr. Heathrow cautioned him not to and to just lie still and try to open his eyes. Everyone was on pins and needles. His eyes began to flutter, and Alford started rubbing his arm.

"That's it, Champ," he said. "You can do it. I'm so proud of you."

His eyes stopped fluttering, and everyone held their breath, afraid he was taking a turn for the worse.

"What's happening with him, Heathrow?" Grayson grumbled.

At the sound of Grayson's voice, Charlie's heart rate elevated. Panic spread across Dr. Heathrow's face as he ran to the machines and grabbed a blood pressure cuff. "His heart rate is increasing, and it seems that his blood pressure is, too," he said. "I need to do a manual read."

Alford knew he needed to stay calm for the family, but he was afraid they had made a big mistake, and these would be the last moments he would have with his son. He moved to the other side of him to make room for Dr. Heathrow. As he did, he noticed Charlie was moving his lips but there was nothing coming out.

"David, get him some water," Alford shouted.

Instantly, Charlie's heart rate slowed, and his blood pressure started to decrease. Dr. Heathrow stared at the monitors and had an idea.

"Keep talking to him Alford," he instructed.

Alford picked up on what he was trying to do and was happy to oblige. "Charlie," he began. "Do you remember our first trip to Utopian together? Do you remember all the plans we had? Well, Champ, you were a part of those plans, and you still are. So, now we need you to do your part. You can do this. You are strong."

He kept talking while Beth helped Charlie get a small drink. If Alford was talking, it seemed as if Charlie was coming out of his state well. He was able to sip some water and keep it down. He moved his mouth again, and this time, a husky whisper escaped. Simultaneously, everyone leaned in to hear again.

"What's that, Champ?" his father asked.

"You were right," Charlie whispered again, his eyes still closed.

"You don't need to try and talk now, son," Dr. Heathrow interjected. "Get some rest and save your strength."

Charlie was persistent, though, and motioned to his father to come closer.

"It's Tate," he said.

"Too late for what, Son?" his father asked.

Charlie's heart rate increased a little, and Dr. Heathrow monitored. "Encourage him to stop talking, Alford."

"No," Charlie managed to say more loudly than anticipated.

Alford leaned closer. "Okay, I'm right here. Go ahead, and then you must rest."

"Tate," he stuttered, "and Grayson ... together ... ring tone and plan," he whispered and then fell asleep.

Alford was trying to piece together what he had just said and make sense of it. Dr. Heathrow assured him that Charlie's vitals were fine and that he was just sleeping. He also said that if Charlie continued to do well, they could head home in two days. Katie had joined her parents, and they were all rejoicing over Charlie waking. Alford hadn't even noticed the concerned glance Grayson gave David as he exited the room.

Grayson didn't even wait until he got to his executive suite; he pulled his phone out as soon as he stepped out of the room.

"Um, sir, I wasn't expecting a call today. We aren't scheduled to talk until Alford returns," the man on the other line said in confusion.

"Shut up, Tate," Grayson snapped. "How stupid could you get? I told you to be careful. The boy is awake, and he knows something is up."

A BIRTHDAY TO REMEMBER

Happy Birthday Dear Charlie, Happy Birthday to you. The small crowd sang in unison as Charlie awkwardly sat at the table in front of a two-tiered chocolate and vanilla cake. This was the tradition that they had every year, and he was grateful that his mother had nixed the sprinkles this time. Truth be told, he had wanted to nix the entire tradition years ago, but he saw how much joy it brought his mother, and he couldn't be the one to end that. Today was a big day for him and not because of his birthday cake but because he was now fifteen, and that meant he could drive if ever his dad needed anything. The family car didn't get out much, so he knew there wouldn't be a lot of time spent behind the wheel, but he was grateful his father had convinced Grayson that this was necessary. He still wasn't sure how that had happened.

The past year since he recovered had been very strange. Grayson had been to Utopian more frequently and seemed to be extra kind to their family. He was even at the party this year and had brought Charlie a gift. He wasn't sure what he was going to use a pocketknife with a window punch for, but it was a gift nonetheless, and he was sure to put on a big show of gratitude. His father had asked him several times about the incident that led to him being rushed to Alpha, but Charlie's memory was so fuzzy. He hadn't even remembered speaking to his father when he came out of the medically-included coma. His father had repeated the words to him over and over, but Charlie was still drawing a blank. His last full memory was of his father leaving for Phoenix.

Dr. Heathrow explained that it could be an adverse side effect of the sedative mixer he had created. He said that, with time, Charlie might recover those memories, or he might never get them back at all. When Charlie heard each of his family members give their side of what happened, though, he was happy he didn't remember.

One thing he did live with was more heart trouble. He found himself out of breath more easily, and it was quite difficult to do the same things he used to. One thing he had been most excited about was the football team, and now his parents were contemplating not letting him join at all. He was devastated, but of course, because of the monitoring, he took the news with a smile and said he understood. What they didn't know is that after he checked in for the night, he had cried himself to sleep. He hated being perfect all the time; the pressure was too much. Since he had returned to Utopian, cheating death, it seemed as if everyone had made him their personal role model. Katie had let it slip that he was the only one in town who hadn't gotten a mark, so he felt like he was under a microscope even more, which he wouldn't have thought possible. The pressure was too much, and sometimes, he just wanted to do one bad thing and get it out of his system. He couldn't though. He wanted to make sure he always made his father proud. Every night before bed, he would look at his family photo on the wall and say, "It's all for you father."

In the past year, he and his father had gotten even closer than before, and his father had shared more details of their past life and how and why they joined Grayson's team. He was finally told about Avery, but his father cautioned him to not mention it to Katie. She was still younger, and he didn't think she could handle it emotionally. Charlie was barely able to handle it. He saw the despair in his father's eyes when he spoke of her—a despair that he had seen a lot more over the last year, though he didn't know why it was there. This only strengthened his desire to be good for his father. So, he took the pressure and dealt with it. His mother interrupted his thoughts with a kiss on the top of his head, tears falling onto his now shaggy dirty blonde locks.

"Oh, Mom," Charlie said. "Lipstick and tears, that's new. I think I'm good with the hair gel."

She ruffled his hair and chuckled. "I know, I know. My baby boy is growing up and doesn't want his mother to cramp his style."

Everyone laughed at this comment, and Beth just stared in confusion at the crowd.

"Mom," Katie said. "Even I know nobody says that."

The room froze and looked out the window, waiting for a mark. Although she was being innocent, Grayson had cracked down on what constitutes a mark. Disrespect and insubordinate behavior were at the top of his list. They weren't expecting what came next. It sounded like a duck was choking. They all looked toward the living room to see Grayson Jeffers laughing. It was such an unusual sound, and in that moment they all realized they had never heard him laugh before. The entire room erupted in laughter and relief. There was no way Team Alpha could ding Katie for her remark if Grayson himself found it funny. Mother began picking up the plates, and both children immediately got up and began to help her.

"Char," she said. "No, sir. This is your birthday. Go outside and do something. Your sister and I will take care of things in here."

He was so excited and didn't hesitate to take her up on that offer. He hadn't noticed that his father had slipped out of the living room. He thanked everyone for coming and headed outside. He wanted to head to the schoolhouse and see if Coach Sal was there to talk to him about what he could do with the football team that wouldn't be too strenuous on his heart. If they could come up with a safe position for him, maybe his parents would let him play. He opened the door, and the blazing sun hit him in the face. While he enjoyed its warmth, it momentarily blinded him. He put his hands on his forehead to help reduce the sun exposure while he refocused his eyes.

"Happy Birthday, Son," he heard his father say.

He finally got his eyes to focus and couldn't believe it. His father was standing outside in front of a steel blue go-cart. It was in mint condition and had a custom decal on the side that said Char15. He was speechless. He ran over and jumped inside and looked up to his father.

"I know it's not a car; those aren't allowed here," his father said. "But I convinced Jeffers to let you have one of these to scoot around town in. There are some rules, though. This is the New World order, you know. You can't go over twenty miles per hour. You always have to give pedestrians the right of way. You can't go out after dark. Finally, you must take this walkie-talkie with you, so I can always get in touch with you. Understood?"

Charlie jumped out of the driver's seat and threw his arms around his father. "Yes, sir! Thank you, thank you, thank you," he said.

"Now, if you want, go ahead and take her for a spin. Be careful to mind the rules," his father replied.

Charlie didn't hesitate. He turned the walkie-talkie on, cranked the engine, and took off. He didn't know where he was headed, but he was determined to get there. His father watched as he took off down the hill. In that moment, Alford had never felt prouder.

"Newsome, you got a minute?" a voice behind him said.

He hated any exchange he had to have with Grayson. He wasn't thrilled with the frequent check-ins or answering to Sheriff Tate, who was mysteriously missing from the birthday celebration. He was fine with that, though; he hadn't wanted to invite him. But Grayson was persistent. Alford hadn't forgotten what he'd found out about Grayson, but he also hadn't decided what he needed to do. For now, he was just trying to keep Utopian trouble-free and be a good father and husband to his family.

"Well, Grayson, for you, I will make the time," he said, careful to play by Grayson's rules.

"We need to talk about something serious," he said.

Alford could tell by the grave look on his face that it was serious. He motioned him over to the picnic table in the middle of the yard, and they both sat down.

"Do you want Beth to bring us something to drink?" Alford asked.

Grayson shook his head. "No, I'd rather just get to it. I have bad news about Phoenix."

Alford realized that with everything that had happened over the past year he hadn't heard from Bo. He was supposed to be his mentor and check in on him every other month. He felt like a huge jerk and then wondered why Grayson hadn't gotten onto him for that yet. He snapped out of his thoughts and back to the conversation. Grayson hadn't stopped talking, and he wasn't sure what all he missed.

"They just celebrated their one-year anniversary, right?" Alford interrupted.

Grayson stared for a moment. "Yes, I just said that."

Alford looked down at the ground. He had missed some important details. "Sorry, when you said Phoenix, it dawned on me I hadn't heard from Bo this entire year."

"Well don't plan on hearing from him now," Grayson shot back aggressively.

Alford had a sick feeling in his stomach. Grayson had said bad news. Had something happened to Bo?

He had to stop losing focus. He had to know what was going on.

"As I was saying," Grayson said. "They had a situation with the Tankersons. You remember Jonas, correct?"

He didn't give Alford time to reply before he continued, but Alford did remember Jonas. He was Bo's law enforcement and had been kind enough to help out when Charlie went to the hospital. He seemed like a stand-up guy.

"Well," he continued. "He passed away in the line of duty three months ago. It was a tragic accident. He was helping to get an elderly resident's cat out of a tree, lost his footing, fell, and slammed his head on the sidewalk, killing him instantly."

Alford's eyes widened. "Oh my, that's terrible," he said.

"Mr. Newsome," Grayson said. "I'm not done."

Alford didn't think there could something worse than what he just heard, but he was wrong. He shut his mouth and stared back silently, careful not to interrupt again.

"You see, the Tankersons are a great family," Grayson continued. "Their boy is Charlie's age, and their mother is as sweet as your Beth. Jonas was a prime choice when I was creating our list. If you remember, he was one of my picks. What we don't understand is what happened with his son. He was perfect at Alpha, much like Charlie. He aced all the tests, and we knew they were a perfect fit for Phoenix. However, he started acting out. He started with minor things: pulling girls' hair, writing on the desks at the schoolhouse, and being disrespectful to his mom. He was getting frequent marks, and it was putting the whole town on edge. I went and had a family meeting with them and Bo, and for a while, he seemed to straighten up—well, so we thought. Actually, he had found a way to disassemble an old two-way radio and use it as a cloaking device for his chip. He found a way to use the controls and frequencies to mess with the video feed. He would go to his room and lay on his bed looking at the ceiling during non-sleep times. We thought he just liked to meditate. He would do this for an hour or so daily. This went on for a month and during that time is when his father had his accident. While we were scrubbing the data for his dad's death to confirm the story of the elderly citizen, one of our techs saw an anomaly in the video feed code. We traced it to Tommy's chip and sent Bo to investigate. He wasn't in his room like his chip showed. No, he was out throwing eggs at the tree his dad fell from. Once we learned he had tricked the system, we removed all technology from his life. Bo was working with his mom to try and reach him, but once his father was gone, it was a lost cause. His acts become more aggressive, and the final straw happened three days ago. His town was at its final mark, and it had only been a year. Bo had called and pleaded that we make an exception since the majority of the marks were from Tommy. I told him we had to stick by the rules and the contracts. If I make exceptions for one, I'd be doing it for all, and we would wind up back where we were when the US lost its way. I did tell him that I would reach out to you and see if there was something you thought we could do to help Tommy since you have all ages of children here and haven't had an issue like this. Well, I never called because it didn't matter. Tommy set that same tree on fire, which triggered the final mark, and their city alarm went off. Ten hours later the town was ReSet."

Alford didn't know what to say. He laid his head on the table and cried. How could this have happened? He should have thought to check on Bo. This was all his fault. This wasn't supposed to happen. There wasn't supposed to be more death. His town was at the end of its eighth year and was doing great. They barely had any marks for this second cycle, and they were on track to do even better for this five-year phase than they had before. Another ninety-nine people dead. That was not supposed to happen. He immediately thought of Bo—poor Bo. He was glad he was alive. That was the deal with the chairperson; they would be spared, but he couldn't imagine how he was feeling. He loved those people. He realized he was still sobbing in front of Grayson and quickly composed himself. He sat back up, unsure why Grayson was telling him this now.

"It's fine," Grayson said. "This devastated me too. I didn't think that we would ever have to ReSet any of our chosen. We were so careful to pick the good."

Alford remembered that he had told Grayson that it was too soon to start the next city. He had told him that they needed to wait.

"We still have our third city doing well, they also just finished their first year. They're doing great, and we're set to start our fourth city in two weeks. So, lesson learned," Grayson said.

"You're already starting another one?" Alford asked. He couldn't believe it. "What do the remaining hundred people think knowing that Bo's city was just obliterated?"

Grayson's look answered his question.

"They don't know, do they?" Alford asked. "How did you explain Bo being back at Alpha? Why hasn't he reached out to me?"

"I didn't need to explain anything," Grayson replied. "Nobody except my monitoring team, DeeDee, Bo, Judy and Tommy Tankerson, and now you know. They haven't seen Bo. He's staying with DeeDee until after the next city is launched, and then he'll rejoin my team at Alpha. He won't reach out to you because I've instructed him not to."

"Okay then," Alford said. He was unsure how to respond to this. He didn't understand how Grayson was so calm. They had a vision for peace, harmony, and good. He had just wiped out another set of people, and he didn't seem very bothered by it. There weren't many Americans left. He wished Grayson would have done something differently, especially since it was really just one person who had messed up the entire plan.

"So, why exactly are you sharing this with me then?" Alford asked, suddenly aware there was more to this conversation. Grayson wasn't here for a social visit, after all.

"That's what makes you a good chair," Grayson said. "You pick up on things. I had an idea. I want to understand why Utopian was so successful. I don't want our final two cities to meet the same fate that Phoenix and Bo did. So, being as brilliant as I am, I figured out the perfect plan. I spared Judy and Tommy. They will be moved to your city, and you can work with Tommy and make him as good as Charlie."

Alford's jaw dropped. Was he crazy? He couldn't send the boy who single-handedly wrecked an entire town of people to Utopian. Then it dawned on him what he just said.

"So, you are giving the boy a second chance, but you killed the city?" Alford asked.

"Well, I wasn't going to," Grayson said. "They were included in the ReSet. However, I was monitoring the ReSet, and it hit me that the only way to make sure this doesn't happen again is to fix the problem. The only way to fix the problem is to find a way to solve it. That's when I thought of your success and how good Charlie is. You're the key factor in that. So, I had a team run into their house as the gas was filling their rooms. They were on the couch together and the gas was already taking effect. I had my team put oxygen on them and carry them out. They woke at Alpha, and I told them the whole thing. I figure this will also put some scare in Tommy, so I helped you out already. They'll be here at the end of the week, and you'll have the weekend to get them settled before I turn their chips back on."

Alford was beyond mad. He didn't know he could feel another level of hatred toward this man, yet as he sat across him, he could feel the wrath taking over. He envisioned trying to snap his neck right there and ending all this. He wasn't sure how well that would play over since Grayson had been special ops. He knew if he even attempted, Grayson would get one over on him; plus, his family would pay the price. "Grayson," he said. "Let me tell you what I think about this plan." He figured he could at least could give him a piece of his mind, mark or no mark.

A static sound coming from under the table halted him. "Dad, can you hear me? Over," Charlie said on the other end of the walkie-talkie. Alford had already forgotten he gave it to him. He wasn't sure, but it almost sounded like there was something off with his voice.

"Champ, I'm here," he replied. "Are you okay? Over?"

"Dad, come to the park, by the lamp posts," he replied with a tremble in his voice. "It's Sheriff Tate. He's dead."

THINGS CHANGE

Alford sat in the driveway for several more minutes thinking about everything that had happened over the last six months. They had experienced more than their fair share of adventures in their lifetime, but it seemed as if the last six months had surpassed all of their adventures combined. With the addition of Tommy and his mother to their town, everything was a disaster. They also had to have a funeral for the Sheriff, and the mystery of his death was still looming. He was told by Grayson that an autopsy would be ordered, but he hadn't seen any results yet. It was so strange pulling up to that accident with Grayson. It looked as if Tate had lost control of his vehicle and slammed into a tree. Given the fact that he hadn't been wearing his seatbelt, his death was probably instantaneous. The question of what caused the accident to begin with was the part that remained a mystery. That is why an autopsy was needed. In Utopian, there were no other cars on the road and no random stray dogs to dodge. Moreover, nobody drank, so there didn't seem to be an obvious reason he ran off the road.

Although Alford was worried about that, he felt like he needed to prioritize his worries because there were so many of them. Right now, he needed to address the next problem. "We're home, guys," he said. "Wake, Wakey, eggs and bakey."

He could hear the groaning from the back of the car.

"Father," Katie said. "We aren't little anymore."

Alford chuckled to himself. He secretly only still said that to get on his kids' nerves. They used to love it when they were little, but they had made him aware it was no longer cool. He loved moments like this. Moments that made him feel that life was normal and okay. Moments that unfortunately were just a large smokescreen concealing a very serious situation.

"Charlie, take Katie inside and make sure she gets settled," Alford said. "It's late and y'all need to get to bed. Your mother and I will be in soon. I love you both very much."

Charlie was half-asleep, but he picked up on his father's tone immediately. He stared at his father who gave him a gentle nod. Something was on his father's mind, and he didn't like not knowing. He was so worried about his Father as of late, and he knew it was because of Tommy. He couldn't stand Tommy. Charlie had tried for the first month that Tommy was put into Utopian to befriend him. They weren't allowed to tell anybody the real reason the Tankersons were in Utopian, and that made Charlie hate the situation even more. The last thing Charlie wanted to do was add to his father's stress.

"Yes sir," he replied. "We love you too; see you in the morning." He rubbed his mom's shoulder and took his sister by the hand. As soon as the front door was closed, Beth beat Alford to the punch.

"What is it dear?" she asked.

Alford couldn't help but smile. He loved how much his wife loved him. He loved how much they had overcome. He just hoped this wouldn't break them.

"I have to tell you some things I've been keeping to myself," he began. "Some things that have made me re-evaluate our role in Utopian, and ... well, really this whole New World ReOrder." He sucked in his breath and held it, waiting for his wife to erupt.

"Our chips are still off, I presume," she asked, and Alford nodded his head. "Then proceed, dear," she said.

They sat for over an hour, and Alford admitted to everything. He told her about what Grayson had done to Charlie, about Bo not being allowed to speak to them, about David and Tate's weird meetings, and about how things felt different with Grayson. He admitted that he felt like they had made a mistake and that something had to be done. She had cried briefly with the news of Charlie's implant situation. No doubt, she was experiencing some of the same anger he had, but she was doing a better job at keeping it all in. After he was done, they sat in silence for a while longer. She finally grabbed his hand in hers and stared deep into his eyes. She knew he had been under pressure for some time, but this was the first time she had seen the despair in his eyes. It bothered her. "What do you suggest dear?" she asked.

"I don't want to make a move in haste, and I don't have a great plan," he admitted. "I've been thinking about this for over a year now. First, I want to go to Grayson and beg him to reconsider. We won't make it if Tommy doesn't change, and I don't know what else to do to reach him. We've had his family over, and I've given him slack at school, and you've worked with his mother directly, but he's such an angry child. I don't know what else to do. His eyes are dead and empty, and that terrifies me. After I meet with Grayson, I think I'll know more. For now, I'm hoping he takes the Tankersons back to Alpha and that will give us more time. Grayson needs to be stopped, but it won't be easy. However, if something doesn't change with Tommy, we'll all be dead, and it won't even matter."

He didn't mean for the last thing he said to be so grave, but it was as honest as he could be. Tommy had single handedly put more marks on that bar in six months than the entire town had.

"Then it's settled," she said. "You'll go to Alpha tomorrow, and we'll hope that Grayson actually listens to you." She kissed his hand and headed inside to get ready for bed herself. Alford sat a little while longer. He had lied a little; he already did have a plan regarding what to do about Grayson, but it was a suicide mission, and he wasn't ready to tell his wife just yet. Before that, though, he had to make sure Utopian was safe. He had a plan for that, too. He joined his wife inside; he needed a good night's rest before he made the trip to Alpha. He also planned on taking Charlie with him.

"Hey there, Picture-Perfect Charlie," Tommy teased. "Where you headed, Picture-Perfect?" Tommy Tankerson was sitting on top of the picnic table outside the Newsome home.

It was early in the next morning, and Charlie couldn't fathom why he was there. They weren't friends. Charlie had tried that. Charlie didn't think that Tommy actually wanted friends. He cringed every time he saw him. Tommy meant trouble, and trouble was the last thing Charlie wanted right now. He was going to Alpha with his father, and he knew something was up.

"You know that isn't an insult, right?" he asked Tommy. "Being good is what we're supposed to do."

Tommy opened his mouth to say something in rebuttal but couldn't think of anything clever.

"You should be good too, Tommy," Charlie said. "This town is really important to us, and you're a part of this town. You have to be good; lives are literally depending on you right now." Charlie knew what happened to Bo's town, and he knew that Tommy had almost been killed. He couldn't understand why that hadn't scared him into being the perfect little angel.

"Guys like me don't deserve a second chance," Tommy said. For a moment, Charlie saw something he hadn't yet seen in Tommy—sadness. Tommy was always sarcastic and talked a big game. Just then, he looked scared and lonely. Briefly, Charlie felt bad for him, which was a first. Tommy must have felt the shift in Charlie's emotions because he met his gaze and his face scrunched up very tightly "I mean, we don't need a handout from anybody. Guys like me do what we want," he said. "Tommy the Tank does what Tommy the Tank wants." With that, he started walking toward Charlie with his fist clenched. Charlie's eyes widened. Was he about to hit him? Charlie thought of what he could do to rectify the situation before another mark hit the bar. His mind was blank. He closed his eyes tightly, so at least only one side of the punch would show to Alpha. Maybe they wouldn't know. His feed was wonky, but they had gotten really good at unscrambling it in almost real time. Charlie just decided to take it like a man and hope that he could fix it after it was done.

"What's going on out here, boys?" said a familiar voice behind him, and Charlie breathed a sigh of relief.

Tommy had made it right in front of Charlie just when his dad stepped outside. "Oh, nothing, Mr. Newsome," Tommy said. He put his right arm around Charlie. "Just saying hi to my good friend, Charlie."

"Right," Alford said. "Well thanks for stopping by, Tommy. You may want to hurry and get going. Your classes will start soon, and you don't want to be late."

"I figured I would walk with Charlie to class," Tommy said.

"No, not today," Alford replied. "I need to take Charlie to Alpha to have his heart looked at."

Tommy glared at Charlie. He was mad that Charlie got to skip school, certain that he used that stupid heart thing as an excuse to get out of all kinds of things. "Fine," he said. "Charlie, you and I will pick up where we left off as soon as you get back." He turned without waiting for Charlie's response and ran down the hill.

Charlie and Alford both stared at the behavior bar, just waiting. Much to their surprise, nothing happened, and they were relieved. They got in the car and headed down the road. Alpha was a long trip, and Charlie was so excited that he was getting to accompany his dad this time. Alford hadn't admitted it to anyone, but he was secretly afraid to leave Charlie behind. Last time, he had almost lost him. He tried his best to make the trip enjoyable. His wife had packed plenty of snacks, and they took turns telling stories of their favorite memories. However, as much as he was trying to make the trip seem normal, he knew his son was smart. He knew he would want to know the real reason they were going to Alpha. He had told Charlie it was a heart checkup. He had told Grayson that Charlie had been acting funny and he wanted to check him out. He had told David the same thing. Only Beth knew the real reason they were going.

It was nearing midnight when they arrived at Alpha. The removal of the dome wowed Charlie. Alford realized that the last time Charlie had been brought here, it was in the back of an air-medic and he was strapped to a gurney unconscious. The time before that, he had just been a small child and it didn't exist. "It's impressive, isn't it, Son?" he said.

"What is it?" Charlie asked.

"It completely hides Alpha from everyone on the outside," Al said. "It also jams our monitoring chips as soon as it closes again. It's Grayson's latest and greatest in security."

Charlie sat silently as they drove into the entrance bay. Slowly, he heard the deafening metal closing and the darkness surrounding them as the dome shut again. He waited until it was completely dark, with only the headlights offering any light. "It's a bit much, don't you think?" he asked.

His father erupted in laughter. He did think it was too much. It had really shown how far gone Grayson was with his paranoia. Grayson had wiped out the entire United States and then another 100 people and yet with all that power, he was still afraid. Charlie didn't understand what was so funny, but he was glad to see his father laughing. It made him feel good that he had been the one to cause it to happen. They got out of the vehicle. Alford scanned his eyes, and the basement elevator door dinged open. They rode quietly to floor two. The doors opened, and Grayson was waiting.

"There are my two favorite Newsome boys," he said.

Both Charlie and his father exchanged quick glances. Grayson was never jovial.

He walked right between them and put his arms around them.

He was up to something; Alford was sure of it.

"Sorry your heart has been acting up, Charlie," he said. "Dr. Heathrow will check you out in the morning. Please head to your normal bunking station, and we'll catch up in the morning at 07:00 sharp." With that, he disappeared without either one of them responding.

They finished their walk to their bunk, changed, brushed their teeth, and headed to bed without another word. Charlie lay awake. Grayson had said he was sorry that Charlie's heart was acting up. But he felt fine. In fact, he hadn't had any issues in a few months. When his father told him they needed to go to Alpha because of his heart, Charlie didn't argue, but he knew his father was lying to him. They had just gotten back from Phoenix, and now his dad was set on going to Alpha. Charlie was willing to play along for his father's sake, but he wanted to know what was actually going on. He hoped he would get his answers in the morning.

Morning came fast, and Charlie was startled awake by his father. "Char, get up. Get up now," he said. "I need you to do exactly as I say, and please don't question me."

Charlie was wide awake now. What was his father talking about? Why did he look so worried? He sat up in his bed and watched as his father was walking all around the room waving his arm around like a crazy person. "What are you doing?" he asked. His father put his fingers to his lips. Charlie stared in confusion. He finished the last wall of the room and came back to sit on his bed.

"Listen, Char," he began. "I'll tell you everything as soon as I can. For now, I can't. I just need your help."

"What were you doing with your arm?" Charlie asked.

"There isn't time. Grayson will be here soon," his father said.

"Father, make time," Charlie demanded.

"Okay," his father said. "I tweaked my watch and made some improvements. I installed a bug detector. If I push these two buttons on the side together, they activate a scanning program that I can use to make sure there are no listening or recording devices wherever we are. I also can turn on this and can momentarily cause a lapse in the feed that is being sent to Alpha. It's only for three minutes, but it's enough to not cause confusion. Okay. That's all the time we have."

"Why do you need your watch to do those things?" Charlie asked. "When did you do that?"

"While you were sleeping," his father replied. "That's enough questions. Now, get up and do fifty jumping jacks right now. Also, when we're in front of Grayson, say to me that you're remembering something about Sheriff Tate."

Charlie was so confused. His father knew he couldn't do that. That would stress his heart out too much. He was never allowed to do physical activity like that. He saw something strange in his father's face, though, and knew he needed to trust him. So, he did as he was told. Not to his surprise, after just forty-two jumping jacks, his heart was tight, and he felt dizzy and out of breath. He sat down on his bed, and the cold sweat began to pour down his back. It was 7:02 a.m.

"Charlie," his dad asked. "Are you all right, Son?"

Right on cue, Grayson entered the room.

"Help," Alford said. "It's his heart." Grayson ran over, and both men lifted Charlie to his feet. They each put one of his arms around him and began walking him out of the room. "Heathrow is already in the med bay; let's get him there right away."

Charlie was feeling very dizzy and even more confused. What was his dad up to? He felt like he was going to pass out and then remembered what else his father wanted. "Father," he said weakly. "I think I remember something about Sheriff Tate ..." With that, Charlie passed out. It had worked though. Alford saw the fear in Grayson's face. They made it to the med bay, and Dr. Heathrow rushed to their aide. He helped them get him to a table, and he started checking his vitals and hooking him up to a heart monitor.

"He's having an episode, Paul," Alford said.

"Um, Newsome," Grayson said. "I need to, um ... talk to DeeDee. Could you go get her and tell her to come to the med bay?"

"Right now?" Alford gasped. "I'm sorry, sir, but Charlie needs me."

"Yes, now," Grayson said. He tried to mellow his tone. "It's very important to me, and Dr. Heathrow will look after Charlie."

Alford leaned over to Charlie and kissed him on the top of the head. He whispered that everything was okay and that he would be back soon. He ran out of the med bay and toward the service elevator.

As he got on and the doors shut, he dropped his head to avoid the cameras and smiled. His plan was working. He got off the elevators and gave the message to DeeDee. She was in the middle of carrying something into the closet for Grayson, and Alford offered to finish it for her. He explained that Grayson said it was emergent. She agreed and handed him the box of file folders and she ran to the elevator. He walked toward the closet and smiled at her as the elevator doors shut. As soon as the elevator was moving down, Alford threw the box in the closet and ran to DeeDee's desk. He pulled a thumb drive out of his pocket and inserted it into the computer.

"Come on, come on," he whispered. "Please load. Aha, yes!" he said. He looked at DeeDee's computer screen, and the security feed had ReSet to him running toward the elevator; now it was empty as if nobody was there. He couldn't believe his software had beat Grayson's firewall. That was a huge risk. He ran back to the mainframe closet and lifted his watch to the door. He hadn't told Charlie about this feature. The watch scanned the locking device and shot a four-digit code across its screen. Alford punched it in and heard a tinkling sound. Okay, one more step. The eye scanner. Alford pulled up a picture of Grayson on his watch and zoomed into his eye. He looked around to make sure that the elevator wasn't moving. He knew they would be expecting him back any second. He had to hurry. He held his breath, and after a few seconds heard another tinkling sound and then the release of the door lock. He was in! He had one shot—one chance. He better not screw it up. He ran to the mainframe and did a search for Utopian. He waited as the computer trilled, and finally, all of the files started uploading. He checked his watch. He probably only had two more minutes before someone would be suspicious. All of the files were finished. He pulled out another thumb drive and inserted it into the computer. He tapped his fingers nervously on the desk. 72% complete, nearly there.

"What do you think you're doing?" he heard behind him. He hadn't even noticed that somebody had entered the room.

KEEP YOUR FRIENDS CLOSE

Alford felt the hair stand on his neck. He had known this was a gamble, but he had convinced himself he had run every scenario and it would work. He shouldn't have been so confident. What was going to happen to his family? How did he not hear someone come into the room?

"Are you crazy, Al?" a familiar voice rang out again. "What are you doing in the mainframe? And where is Grayson? We're supposed to have a meeting in five minutes."

He turned to face David King. Immediate relief flooded his body, but fear quickly followed. He still wasn't sure he could trust David anymore, and they hadn't been the same in years. He glanced back down at the drive. Only twelve percent left to go. He ignored David and went back to what he was doing. He started typing on the computer. He needed to install a cloaking firewall, to ensure that if a cleaning scan was run on the computer, there would be no trace of any foreign entities. His fingers were moving faster than they had ever moved before.

"Are you seriously going to ignore me?" David said. He waited a few more moments and went straight to Alford just as the drive was finishing. Alford pulled it out and stuffed it into his pocket. David grabbed him by the shoulders, turned him around, and pushed him out of the room. Alford ran back to DeeDee's computer and stuck the thumb drive in again. This time, he was setting things back on her computer. He looked at his watch, set a timer, and dragged David to the elevator and coaxed him inside. He had planned this out perfectly and he didn't need David's unexpected presence messing up everything he had calculated. He pushed the basement floor sending a very confused David away. He had hoped that after all they had been through, he would keep his mouth shut if he ran into Grayson. He ran back to the closet where he had originally been and looked at his watch. As soon as it went off, he started slowly walking toward the elevator. He pushed the button and when the door opened, David King was still there. He got on the elevator, and they rode down in silence. As they reached the bottom, David stopped the elevator and entered a code. "I disabled the camera, Al," he said. "Spill, now."

"I can't tell you anything. It's for your own good," he said. He tried to push the button to start the elevator again, but David grabbed his arm. "Now," he said. It was clear to Alford that he wasn't going to pretend like he hadn't seen what he did. He tried to think how he could explain this away.

"You can trust me," David said.

Alford looked him dead in the eye. "Can I?" he asked. It just came out. He had wanted to ask him that for a long time.

David looked genuinely pained at the doubt he saw in his friend. They had been through so much together, and the Newsomes were his family. "How could you even ask that?"

"Really!" Alford replied. "There's no question about it, David. Things have been weird between us. Meanwhile, you've gotten closer to Grayson, who may I add has done some very questionable things lately. Did you know about him being the one to implant Charlie? Did you know he made Paul Heathrow take the blame? Did you know that he ReSet Phoenix but saved the boy who caused their downfall? Did you know that he won't let Bo even call me? Did you know he put Tommy in our town, and I'm terrified that we're next to be destroyed? Did you know that I think that is his plan to get rid of me? I think he feels threatened or something ..." It felt good to get all this off his chest. He hadn't planned on this meeting with David, but he had been holding so much in for so long, it felt nice to let it all go. He realized that David hadn't said anything yet and was quickly reminded that he may have just ruined everything by purging in this manner. He was supposed to be coming up with a plan to pacify David. He stopped talking to give David a second.

"You forgot something, Al," David said. "Did you know that he had Sheriff Tate killed?"

Alford's jaw dropped. Had he heard his best friend correctly? How did he know this information? David too looked relieved. "Dr. Heathrow and I had lunch the other day. He's been different since everything happened with Charlie last year, but I wasn't sure why. He does really good putting on a front in front of Grayson, but I knew something was up. He told me everything. He also told me that Grayson told him not to do an autopsy on Tate. He said that it was natural causes, and there was no need to waste resources on it. So, Heathrow did it anyway. When he examined the contents of his stomach, there were only three things: coffee, creamer, and ricin. Heathrow thinks there must have been powdered ricin mixed in with his creamer. He had been ingesting it daily. It would have caused his organs to fail, and he either passed out or died in the car while driving, which caused him to run into that tree."

"How do you know it was Grayson?" Alford said. "And why would he do that?"

"Well, he was here a few days before his accident. He made trips here often for, um meetings. At the last meeting, DeeDee gave him a gift basket. It had coffee, creamer, sugar, and cookies in it. He joked with me on the elevator that he was surprised the old dog had given him anything, since he had messed up so badly." David looked down after biting his lip. He couldn't even face Alford.

"You bit your lip, David," Alford said. "What is it?"

David looked up with tears in his eyes. "He made me do it and I'm so sorry, Al," he cried. "Listen, he was afraid you were losing your loyalty, so he had me and Tate spying on you. I don't know what Tate did, but Grayson said he'd come really close to messing everything up. I heard him tell Tate at one of the meetings that he should have been more careful, especially around that Newsome boy. I don't know what that means, I promise. I was never told anything about Char or Katie. I was just told that he was afraid you weren't on board, and he wanted to make sure. We are supposed to all be in this together for the greater good, remember?" David was sobbing now.

"What does my son have to do with?" asked Alford, then stopped, as it hit him like a ton of bricks. He pulled his watch out and scrolled up through his screen. "That's it!" "Tate, phone, Grayson. Grayson has been calling Tate. He has that special ring tone. Charlie must have heard it that day, saw Tate, and realized that he was some type of mole. He was so young and probably terrified that it sent him into a heart attack!" He shut his eyes, gritted his teeth, and clinched his fists.

"I had no idea," David said. "I'm so sorry. I didn't know what to do. You have to believe me. I would never hurt your family intentionally."

"I do believe you," Alford said. "Grayson has gone too far. If we want to set things right and have a chance of truly making this world great again, we have to get Grayson out of the picture."

"What do you mean?" David asked.

"I don't know. I'm still working it out," Alford said. "For now, I have to get back to Charlie. They have to wonder what's taking so long. I also have to get home and make sure Utopian is safe. I have a plan, but it's going to take about a year. I have to try and convince Grayson to take Tommy back or we may not make it. David, are you in or out? You have to choose a side."

David looked at Alford. This was his friend. This man had never done anything to harm him and had always been there for him. He was torn because he felt like Grayson had done the same thing in the beginning. However, he knew that Grayson had gone dark. He kept telling himself that he was no different than the people he said had ruined the US. After all, he had killed Tate for self-preservation. Alford was right, something had to be done. He took a deep breath in and exhaled. "What do you need from me?" Alford smiled and gave him a famous Bo Bear Hug.

The two men walked down the hall and into the med bay room. Alford had very quickly planned an explanation for why he had been gone so long. He needed David with him as part of his cover. As he entered the room, he was happy to see Charlie sitting up sipping from an apple juice box. "Hey, you're up, Char!" Alford said. He ran over and kissed his son on the top of his head.

"Yes, we were just having a nice chat," Grayson interrupted. "So, you're saying you don't remember what you were saying right before you blacked out?" Grayson looked uncomfortable, as did DeeDee.

"No sir, not really," Charlie said. He looked toward his father, trying to desperately read his mind. "I was thinking about Sheriff Tate, I know that. I think it had something to do with the crash, but I am not sure now, I'm sorry." He began sipping his drink again.

"Can you tell what is going on with him, Paul?" Alford asked.

"It looks like he's been doing pretty good, considering," Paul said. "This may just be a one-off. Maybe you're getting good at picking up warning signs. It was good that you were already here. This was a mild one, though. He should be good in a couple of hours to head back home." He extended his hand to shake Alford's. Alford returned the shake and mouthed "thank you" to him. Paul nodded his head and checked Charlie's vitals one last time.

"Look who I found getting in the elevator as I was getting off," Alford said. "I was able to tell him why we were here, and he wanted to come check on Charlie."

"Uncle Dave," Charlie said. "I haven't seen you in so long."

Charlie and David caught up as DeeDee and Grayson exited the room. Alford followed. "Grayson," he began. "I was hoping to talk with you a minute, now that Charlie is fine."

"DeeDee, please do what I asked," Grayson said. "I'll be up there in a minute."

The two men stayed in the hallway as Alford explained to Grayson everything that was going on at Utopian. He knew that there was no doubt Grayson had been following along closely, but he wanted to give him his side personally. He begged Grayson to let the Tankersons come back to Alpha, to save his town. He had decided that this was Grayson's final chance to do what was right. He told Grayson that he was sure that if he didn't let Tommy leave Utopian, Utopian would be gone within the year. Grayson waited before responding, and Alford thought for a second he had convinced him. Maybe he was wrong about Grayson. Maybe the guy he had met all those years ago who believed in making the right decisions for the good of all mankind was still in there.

"No, Newsome," he replied. "You have to find a way to fix Tommy. There very well could be more Tommy's in the future, sadly. We have to know the solution."

Alford dropped his head. So much for that. Grayson no longer had any good in him. Then, Al had an idea. "In that case, I need help," he said.

Grayson looked genuinely intrigued. "What do you mean?"

"Helping Tommy is going to be a full-time job. If you want me to do it, you need to help me. I need someone I trust to run Utopian while I focus on fixing Tommy. Someone who knows how I think. Someone I can work well with."

Grayson raised one eyebrow suspiciously. "I'm guessing you have someone in mind."

Alford paused and changed his answer. "Yes, Bo. I want to talk to him. I want to give him a second chance."

"Not Bo," Grayson said. "You can see Bo before you leave and say hi, but he isn't going with you. You can take Mr. King."

"I suppose he'll be fine," Alford said. Inside he was beaming. That is exactly who he wanted, but he knew Grayson had to feel like it was his idea. Grayson said he was heading to his office and told David to join him. As David walked by, Alford bit his own lip. He never did this, but he knew David would catch on. He would understand that their plan was beginning. He did trust him, and he was glad to have his friend back again. Now that he had Grayson's permission, he called Bo and asked him to come to the med bay. Charlie had fallen asleep, and Dr. Heathrow said he would be fine to travel in an hour or two but to let him get his rest. Alford went to the waiting room to get a cup of coffee. Within ten minutes, Bo was there, and they were exchanging hugs and laughs. Alford apologized to Bo for everything that had happened. He told him he was a bad friend. Bo told him he understood he had a lot going on and didn't blame Alford one bit. He said he was very upset that Grayson had destroyed all those good people. He was surprised to find out that the Tankerson boy and mom were spared. Alford hadn't meant to reveal any secrets; he'd been sure that Bo knew. Why hadn't Grayson told him?

They sat in silence for several minutes.

"What are you boys talking about?" Dr. Heathrow asked. He walked into the breakroom, poured a cup of coffee, and joined the men. Alford had always liked Paul, but he didn't know if he could trust him. He knew that Paul had been worried since he told one of Grayson's secrets that Alford would rat him out, so he was sure he was just checking in to make sure all was well. He also knew that Paul had no way of knowing that Alford knew about Sheriff Tate. He was also now sure that poor Bo was just an innocent bystander in all of this.

"Nothing much. Just catching up," Alford lied.

Paul looked behind him and inched closer to both the men. "Guys, I think we have to do something about Jeffers." He leaned back in his chair and took a sip of his coffee.

Alford was dumbfounded. That was the last thing he had expected.

"We're all a part of the beginning of this thing. We all had the vision, but I think the power has gone to Grayson's head. He's doing terrible things. He's made me his cover guy and his fall guy, and I can't take it anymore. I'm not this person. I'm a good person."

Bo looked at Paul and shrugged his shoulders. "I mean, I just heard about the Tankerson thing, but I'm sure he had his reasons, fellas," he said.

Alford shook his head. Poor, poor Bo. He had no idea. Alford realized that not only did he have David, but he now had Dr. Heathrow. He could be his inside guy. It wouldn't hurt having Bo on his side too. He also felt like he owed it to Bo to make sure he was on the right side of things when they went sideways, which he knew was inevitable. "Bo," he said, "let me fill you in on some things ..."

He quickly went back and told him everything he knew. When he got to the part about the sheriff's death, Dr. Heathrow looked shocked. He hadn't told Alford, so he wasn't sure how he knew about it. After Alford had finished, Bo sat back and folded his arms. He looked up at the ceiling tiles and sighed. Alford let the room go silent. He knew Bo had a decision to make, he was risking everything by putting his trust in him. He wasn't sure he had done enough to convince him. "Look fellas," he began. "I don't know about all this. I don't feel like this is right. I think we need to get Grayson's side to all this." He stood to exit, and Alford's heart dropped into his stomach. He had made a big mistake in telling Bo. He didn't know what to do. He had been sure he could convince Bo to be on their side.

"Bo," Dr. Heathrow said. "He killed Thad and Tracy too."

Bo stopped, turned back around, and sat down. "Come again," he stuttered.

Dr. Heathrow dropped his head and sobbed. "I had no part in it, but I know that he did."

Alford was confused. He didn't know who these people were.

"My adopted parents?" Bo questioned. "No sir, that's not what I was told. That's not what you said. You told me they both had contracted some type of bacteria that caused some type of organ failure. I was with them. I watched them get sick. I was there, Doc. I held their hands for their last breath."

"It was a lie that Grayson made me tell you," Dr. Heathrow said between tears. "He told me that your parents weren't supposed to be here. He said you made him bring them and he didn't like ultimatums. He said that they went against the plan and if people found out how they got here everyone would go against the system and there would be mutiny and everything we did, all those people who died, it would have been in vain. I didn't do anything to them, I just lied about it. Bo, I'm so sorry."

Bo stood there, unable to move. His eyes were ablaze with anger. Alford understood that look. "You helped me bury their ashes. Grayson built those crosses for their graves," Bo said with disdain.

"I know," Dr. Heathrow said. "I felt it was the least I could do. He used ricin, just like he did for Tate. I told you, he's gone too far. He had me convinced it was the only option."

Alford knew he needed to say something before Bo burned the whole place down. "Listen, Bo, there is one person to blame here. Only one. I have a plan, but I need all the help I can get. If we act on our emotions alone, a lot more innocent people will die. You don't want that. This needs to stop now."

That was exactly what Bo needed to hear. His face went calm, and he sat back down. Alford knew Bo was on their side—this time for sure. "You and Dr. Heathrow need to stay here. I need men on the inside. You have to act like all is okay. Distance yourself from him if you need to. Just wait for more instructions." Bo and Heathrow shook their heads.

"Father," Charlie cried out. The three men stood up and looked at each other. There was a silence between them, but their expressions said more than enough. They went to Charlie's room, happy to see him up. They helped Charlie out of bed just as Grayson and David came back.

"Bo," Grayson said. "You're here."

"Yes, sir," Bo said. "Just wanted to check in on my pal Charlie. I'll be going now. It was good to see you for a minute, Al. Charlie, you take it easy now, you hear?" Charlie smiled and nodded his head. With that, Bo left without another word. Alford was relieved.

"Well, I've done all I can," Dr. Heathrow said. "Charlie, you know where I am if you need anything." He patted Charlie on the back and left too.

"Well, I guess you three better head back to Utopian. You have work to do." Grayson commanded. Unlike the other two, he didn't say anything to Charlie before exiting. Once Charlie was sure that Grayson was gone, he looked back to his father. He had some serious questions.

"Son," Alford said. "Uncle Dave is with us now, you understand?"

Charlie did, and he was relieved. He had grown very fond of David King through the years. "Yes, sir. I think I do." The three walked toward the elevator in silence. They exited the basement and got back in the car. Right before the dome began to open, Charlie interrupted the silence.

"Father," he said. "How did I do?"

"You did good, Champ," he replied. "Really, really good."

UNDERGROUND CITY

With their monitoring chips in full effect, the car ride home was mostly silent. Each person in that car had so much running through their minds, they welcomed the silence. Alford kept promising everyone he would come up with some sort of plan. He hoped he could come up with something that would solve all the problems they were facing; but he was terrified. Terrified to face the most powerful person left in the United States and perhaps the world. He couldn't wait to fill Beth in on everything that had happened, although he didn't think she was going to be pleased with the whole Charlie situation. He had spoken to Dr. Heathrow extensively about Charlie's limitations, so he knew he wasn't putting Charlie in any real danger. He knew that Charlie would just end up feeling exhausted. He was proud that Charlie had played his part so brilliantly. He also knew it was time to make sure Charlie knew everything that was going on. He was still young, but Alford needed as many allies as he could get. Truth be told, part of this plan was recruiting even more from the only place he could. His town. His people. Utopian.

The car pulled into the driveway, and Beth ran to meet him. Her hair was disheveled, and she looked as if she hadn't slept in the last two days. He got out of the car very quickly and ran to meet her.

"Oh, Al, we didn't know what to do!" she said. "He just wouldn't stop."

He knew exactly what she was talking about and looked toward the behavior bar on the closest billboard. Sure enough, it had gone up three points in two days. It was a new record.

"Do you know where he is?" Alford asked. Beth shook her head no. He pushed the hair off her face and tucked it behind her ears. He kissed her forehead, trying to reassure her that things would be okay. She saw right through him, and he knew it.

"Listen," he said softly. "David is here to help now. Everything is going to be fine. Everything is under control. I have a plan, and it will all work out. Please set up the guest room for David, and Charlie and I will go find Tommy. He was hoping she was reading between the lines. He needed to get started as soon as possible. Time was of the essence."

Charlie and his father got in the car and headed toward town. Alford had asked Charlie to go find Tommy and invite him and his mother to dinner. He needed to go and let the town know that there would be a town meeting the following evening and everyone must be in attendance. Charlie wasn't happy with the plan, but he could feel something big was changing, and he knew his father needed his full support. Besides, he was pretty sure he knew where Tommy was.

***

It didn't take him long to find him. He was exactly where he thought he was going to be.

"Tommy, can we please talk?" he called out.

"What do you want, Picture-Perfect?" Tommy called out. He didn't bother standing up. He was still sitting propped up against the bleachers. He looked sick.

"Tommy," Charlie started. "Why did you get three marks?"

"Man, just leave me be," Tommy said. "Why do you care what I do with my life? Go back to your picture-perfect life and family and just let me be."

"Don't you get it?" Charlie said. "How can you not get it? What you do affects my life. It affects all our lives. Every time you get a mark, our chance of dying increases. You've already increased it more than we have ever seen, and this city has been here almost ten years. You've been here six months!"

"I'm sorry, okay," he almost yelled. It wasn't an angry yell—more depressive than anything. "I can't be you. I can't be good like you. I just can't. You would never understand. He dropped his head between his knees and didn't say anything else."

"Can you just, I don't know, try?" Charlie asked. Tommy didn't acknowledge him in any way. "Look, my father said there is a town meeting tomorrow night at 5 p.m. Everyone has to be there. We would also like to have you and your mom over for dinner tonight. Please tell her, and please come. It would mean a lot to us." Charlie waited a second longer, kicking his feet in the dirt waiting to see if Tommy would say anything. He waited a few more seconds with no response. "Okay, then. I'm going to go. Please come, though." Charlie turned to leave, confident he hadn't gotten through to Tommy. He couldn't understand how one person could be so selfish.

***

Dinner came and went, and there were no Tankersons present. Nobody was surprised.

There were hushed whispers throughout the entire town hall. Most of the city had shown up early in hopes of getting a private chat with Mr. Newsome. They were disappointed when he showed up right at 05:00 p.m. He got onto the stage and the entire room shushed simultaneously. He looked around at the people he had grown to love, and his heart was heavy. He had to save these people—his people. He welcomed David King back to Utopian and explained to everyone that he would be joining the city while they made some changes to help improve things. As he said that, everyone looked around. Everyone was looking for two people—the two people who needed to be there the most but that were the most unwelcomed. Sure, everyone treated them wonderfully, because they didn't have a choice, but inside they all wished the Tankersons had never shown up. It was tragic really because Mrs. Tankerson was a gem, and she made the best key lime pie.

One good thing that the town had done was improve their behavior. Collectively, they hadn't ever really gotten many marks, but now they were almost non-existent. Everyone had quickly realized that with Tommy in town, there was no room for anyone else to make a mistake. Quite frankly, the whole town was living on pins and needles. Much to everyone's surprise, the back door opened, and Mrs. Tankerson and Tommy slipped into the meeting and sat in the back row. This was the first meeting everyone had ever been to. Mr. Newsome looked at this as a ray of hope. He greeted them warmly and continued the meeting. "As I was saying," he continued. "We will now be having weekly town cookouts hosted at each family's house so we can all grow as a family. Please sign up on the back-table for the coordinating dates. We will do the first one tomorrow night at my house. These are mandatory for all townspeople, and they are imperative for our survival." With that, he dismissed the town meeting. Several people stayed to stand around and chat. The Tankersons quickly made their exit, and Alford was disappointed. He felt this was their time to bond with the rest of the city. He couldn't spend much time focusing on that, however; he had work to do.

As Grayson watched the town meeting from Alpha, he was hopeful. This was a new and unorthodox approach, but he thought it could work. Maybe all the Tankersons needed was more comradery. Maybe it would pull them into the city and make them feel welcome. Maybe the overwhelming love that Utopian had for each other would spill over and Tommy could change. Grayson felt a sense of pride, though it was misplaced. He had done it. He had found the solution to the Tommy problem, he had pretty much sent Alford's Newsome replacement in already with David King, and nobody suspected a thing. His life was still perfect. Satisfied, he left the monitoring station to go have dinner with DeeDee.

What Grayson Jeffers didn't know was that Alford had devised a plan. Alford had been perfecting the technology for a while now. He had written code to stop a chip's feed for moments at a time, he had written code to relay code that appeared to be something it wasn't, and he had even learned how to terminate the code once and for all—when the time was right. The reason he had needed to get into the mainframe room a few days before at Alpha was that he needed everyone's chip IDs. He was given a list that corresponded to each citizen's name, but the last four digits of each were hidden, and he needed the full codes. This was his entire purpose for getting into the Alpha mainframe room; he needed to download them, as this was the only place they were located. The only thing he hadn't figured out how to do was the one thing he wished he could do the most, and that was stop Charlie's feed without hurting him. He had learned that if he put Charlie into a metal box, he could stop the chip's feed without disabling the chip. It wasn't ideal, but it would at least buy him time and keep Charlie safe. What Grayson Jeffers saw as backyard food and fun, Alford was using as clandestine meetings to try and convince his town that Jeffers was evil and needed to be stopped. At each meeting, he would enter the code on his watch to turn on his three-minute jammer. He used those quick three minutes to tell each citizen that he needed to meet with them at midnight on specific dates so he could fill them in. He told each of them it was imperative that they didn't tell anybody at all and that they didn't act any different. He assured each one that he had found a way to make their feed appear as if they were still in bed asleep. He could tell each person he spoke to was overwhelmed with what they were being told, confused as to how he was doing what he said he could, but completely trusting of the man they were speaking to. He had spent nine years building their trust, and now it was paying off.

Alford was having midnight meetings every night with the Utopianites. He was able to fully explain what had gone on, what he had discovered, and the monster Grayson Jeffers had grown to be. Most of the people were devastated and eventually disgusted. However, most of them had confided in Alford that they were secretly terrified of Grayson and were more fearful for their life because of Tommy and would do anything to support Alford to ensure their own safety. It took him roughly two months to cycle through everyone in the city. The only ones he left out were the Tankersons. He had already resolved himself that he would save them, but he couldn't trust Tommy enough to let them in on the plan. He was gaining more confidence with his plan as each day progressed. He had convinced each person that they would build a new city, an underground city to keep them safe. He had resolved himself that they would never make it to another ReFresh. So, instead of hoping for the best, they had to be proactive. To that end, they were going to build an underground city with several entrance points all over the city. They would stock it full of supplies. He explained to everyone it wouldn't be somewhere they could live forever, but it would be somewhere they would stay until he could find a way to get the other two key cities to them and then ultimately take over Grayson and Alpha. They would need to stay underground until he could ensure everyone would be safe, and he just didn't know how long that would take. Luckily, Grayson had equipped the cities with not only good people but smart people from all kinds of occupations. He had architects, plumbers, contractors, and much more in his city. He had everything he needed to be successful.

Now, they just needed to work—and work quickly. This proved difficult since they had to do everything at night. Around 11 p.m. to midnight each night, he would switch the chips to the people he needed to cover mode, and they would get to work. The hardest part was creating the entrance points all over the city. They knew a ReSet would come, but they just didn't know where everyone would be.

It was mandatory that everyone create openings to the underground city, which they called Undertopian, in the closets of their home. In addition to that, they tasked their town architect to create unique openings all over the city. There were hidden passages in sewer mains, standing post office boxes, the large dumpster behind the library, and in one of the park lamp posts. Each secret passage was set up to open on its own if and when the city alarm sounded and close again exactly ten minutes after the alarm started. Alford had stressed to everyone that no matter what time of day it was, they had to get to an entrance. Everything would be locked out exactly ten minutes after the alarm sounded to ensure that Alpha's ReSet team would have no idea how or where anyone was. Each passageway would have to be sealed from the outside in to ensure their safety. Alford felt like he had thought of everything. It was actually beautiful to see everyone working together in this way. This is why he loved his people. His family had been the most supportive and helpful. He could tell Katie was scared, but she put on a brave face despite it.

The hardest thing for everyone was acting as if everything was normal, knowing what they were doing. The parents knew better than to tell the young children, knowing they wouldn't be able to keep it a secret. They knew it would be up to them to ensure their children made it to the escape points when the alarm sounded. David King had been tasked with getting the Tankerson family into Undertopian when the time came. Alford and Beth would be busy getting everyone checked in and then getting their chips turned off. They wouldn't have much time, and it would take their entire focus. They had already told their children that they were to meet at Charlie's special box. Charlie was to go straight there and get inside the box, just until his dad could figure out how to safely disable his chip. Charlie hated that he wouldn't be able to do more, but he understood. Much to Alford's surprise, the city project was coming together, and they had only been working on it for about eight months. The city was changing, and their lives were changing, but the one thing that was remaining unchanged was Tommy's bad behavior. The bar was at 90 percent and Alford knew their time was almost up.

ONE WRONG MISTAKE

Alford stared at the lamppost on the east side of the park for several minutes. He couldn't believe it! They had done it. Undertopian was complete. He was so proud of his town. They had done the unthinkable in such a short time. David had teased him throughout the whole process, saying that there was no possible way that they could pull it off without Grayson catching wind. David was wrong, though. They had.

In fact, Grayson had called David several weeks ago confirming he was completely in the dark as to the switch. He was going over plans with David on how to remove Alford. He had promised David no harm would come to the family. Grayson expressed he simply thought it best that the Newsome family come back to Alpha. He was also concerned as to why the cookouts weren't working with Tommy. David felt sick to his stomach pretending that he was against the Newsomes. Now that he knew all of Grayson's sordid secrets, he felt disgusted that he was ever a part of his plan. Spending the last eight months in the Newsome's home had reminded David just how wonderful the family really was. They were the real deal—not perfect but pretty close. Except for Charlie, of course. He was still baffled how that boy had managed to not make one mistake in almost ten years.

Now, as Alford stood before the lamppost in awe, he felt something he hadn't in a long time: peace. This by far was the most complicated entrance that they had done. It was Mick and Sal's idea. They reminded Alford that this was the spot of their nightly run and that many families used the park daily. Alford had agreed it was the perfect spot. He was grateful that the poles had already been so beaten up, it helped to conceal the new crack from where they split the pole for the secret entrance. The sun had set over the trees, and the fog was rolling in. He had always loved the park entrance; it had brought him so much joy. Now with the flickering of the yellow lights and the haze of the fog, he got an eerie feeling from them. It's as if they were warning of the impending doom they would face. He looked back at the billboard near the Willow; it read 99 percent. He sighed deeply. It could literally be any second now. He hoped his plan would work. He hoped he could save them all. He checked his watch and realized it was already past 9:00 p.m. He needed to get home. The big homecoming game was tomorrow, and Charlie had successfully convinced his parents to let him play. His coaches had the idea that if he was the kicker, it would be minimalize the stress put on him. Charlie would have been a bench warmer, as long as his parents said yes, and he got to be on the team. He also hoped they would make it to the game. "Come on, Tommy," he muttered to himself.

***

Charlie woke to the sun hitting his face and the smell of his favorite breakfast food: strawberry-stuffed French toast and bacon. The smile spread across his face. What a perfect way to start his day. He sat up, stretched, and threw his lucky tank top on. He was pumped for the game. He didn't even want to think about how high the behavior bar was. They were only a few weeks away from a ReFresh, and he was optimistic that Tommy wouldn't dare be responsible for the death of another town. He shook Tommy from his mind. He was determined not to let anything ruin his day. The aroma of chocolate cinnamon coffee filled his room. The smell nearly lifted him off his feet. He followed his nose to the kitchen and found the entire family at the breakfast table waiting, including Uncle Dave.

"Morning, Champ!" his father said. "How did you sleep?"

Charlie felt his cheeks redden. He hadn't meant to make everyone wait on him. "Great. Thanks, Father," he replied. "You should have woken me up. I'm sorry."

"Oh, don't you be silly," his mother chimed in. "The star of the team needs his rest."

Charlie blushed again. He wished his family wouldn't make such a big deal. The truth was, that the football team was really just a very small flag football team and they played against their own friends because there was no one else to play. Mick and Sal said they would run things as if they had a team of one hundred and everyone should play the same. Charlie took his seat at the table. He looked at the plate his mother placed in front of him, and he could practically feel the drool dripping from his mouth. She winked at him, and he began.

Everyone joined in. For the next thirty minutes, the family talked, laughed, and shared memories. In that moment, life was grand. Charlie sat back in his chair, his stomach full, and thought to himself that his family was kinda picture-perfect. He immediately felt a sadness for Tommy. He had no idea where that had come from; Tommy had made his choice, and he couldn't believe he was feeling sorry for him. He brushed the thought away again. He helped his sister clean the kitchen, got permission to head to the practice field, kissed everybody goodbye, and left. This day was going to be the best day. He needed one of those. The underground city was completed, and his father was at ease.

Charlie spent the next several hours at the field practicing. Coach Mick and Sal had shown up and given him some more pointers. He had lost track of time and needed to go shower before the game. He knew the whole town would be there—well, the ones that mattered. He wasn't expecting Tommy to be there, and he was fine with that. Charlie jumped in his go-cart and headed home. It wouldn't be long now.

Tommy Tankerson had been watching Charlie practice. He didn't understand why Charlie got everything. He had the perfect family, and his father was in charge of the place. He had a cool go-cart, the prettiest girl in school liked him, he was on the team, and he was so stinking perfect. It made him so mad. He balled his fists and prepared himself to punch a hole in whatever he could, but something stopped him. He looked at the billboard: 99 percent. He slowly unclenched his fists. He really didn't want to put another mark on there. He secretly felt bad that he had already caused so much damage. He didn't really intend to get it that high, he just had a hard time controlling himself. He hated himself for the fact that Phoenix had been ruined because of him. All those people gone. He was mad that Grayson had saved him. He was grateful he had saved his momma, though. He loved his momma, but even she hadn't been the same since his papa died and the Phoenix incident. They hadn't talked about it one time. It was too much pressure for him. He had just turned seventeen, and he needed an outlet. Truth be told, as much as he loved his momma, he couldn't face her. If she ever found out his secret; she would never speak to him again. Thinking about how much he had lost so quickly was more than he could bear, and he felt a tear roll down his cheek, which for him only intensified his anger. He had to calm down. He had to go do something, or he knew there would be another mark on that bar. He really was trying to do his best to be good so this town would make it to their next ReFresh. He didn't want any more bloodshed on his hands.

The Newsomes had just made it to the stadium and were standing outside the gate. Beth took Katie by the hand and told Alford she would go save some seats. David was checking in with Mick and Sal to ensure they didn't need anything before the big game.

Alford put his arm around his son and sighed. “Well, Champ,” he said. “This is it. No matter what happens, I’m proud of you, and I love you, Son. You are my joy, and it’s been a privilege being your father.”

Charlie felt the tears in his eyes. His father’s simple words were overwhelming because he could tell his father was talking about more than football. Charlie understood. The idea that Tommy could go another three weeks and not make another mistake was laughable. Honestly, they were both surprised he had gone this long. It was a record for him. Three days and no mark. They knew he must be boiling over. The sound of the small band began to fill the air, and Charlie knew it was time. He hugged his father tightly and ran onto the field.

***

The game should have been an easy win for Charlie’s team. These boys practiced with each other daily and Charlie had learned their every move. It must have been what he saw running into the stadium. That had to be it. It was all Sue’s fault. Sue Sanderson was the prettiest girl in the whole school and Charlie had had a crush on her since the second grade. A crush he had kept to himself until last week. He had heard from her best friend, Chole, that Sue had a crush on Charlie, too. He was over the moon. He had planned on asking her to ice cream after the game. However, as he entered the stadium, he saw Sue in the bleachers talking with Tommy. Tommy of all people. She was giggling and twirling her hair. What was she thinking? She knew better. How could a girl like her get mixed up with the one person who would more than likely be the reason she would die before her eighteenth birthday? Tommy made direct eye contact with him and smiled. He was doing it on purpose. Charlie felt an anger inside him that didn’t happen very often. The thought of punching Tommy straight in his stupid face instantly crossed his mind. But unlike Tommy, Charlie cared about the citizens and instead decided to put his energy into winning the game.

Well, that plan didn't work.

"Hey bud," his sister interrupted his thoughts. "Don't even worry about it. You were still the best-looking out there, even if you lost."

He tried to manage a smile. He knew his sister was trying to lift his spirits, and usually, she could. It wasn't working this time, though. He just felt broken.

"Guys, if it's okay," he said. "Could I just walk home by myself? I'm gonna talk to the coaches, put my gear up, and head home in about twenty minutes. I think I just want to be alone."

His mother opened her mouth to object, but his father put his hand around her and interjected. "That'll be just fine, Champ," he said.

With that, the Newsome family and David King headed up the road toward the house on the hill. Charlie just stood there for a minute watching them and then did exactly as he said he would. The stadium had cleared, and the lights were off. Charlie headed home but decided to take a detour. He wasn't quite ready to face his family yet. He was nearing the fork to head home and stopped near the old marketplace. It closed early each night and the place was dark. He sat on the patio in front of it and hugged his knees. He put his head down on his knees and began to weep. It was too much. It all had become too much. He hated what Grayson had done with the Tommy situation. He hated that the world had ended in the first place and these people were stuck in this dark hole pretending to be normal. He hated that despite how wonderful the town really was, even if they could make it to the next ReFresh, this was all his life would ever be. Mostly, he hated that everyone expected him to be perfect. Did they realize how big of a task that was? Did they realize how unfair it was that they all got to make mistakes, but he didn't and hadn't? What was it all for? There was no way there were making it to a ReFresh, all because of Tommy. He hated Tommy. His mother had taught him that hate was a special evil and that he should never feel that way about someone, but he couldn't help it. Tommy was too much. It was all too much.

"Aggghhh," he screamed out into the darkness. Charlie gasped. He couldn't believe it. He didn't mean to. He didn't even realize the white rock was in his hand. He didn't even remember picking it up off the ground. The shattering of the glass was real, though. He ran to the window and looked inside and there it was. One shiny, white rock the size of the palm of his hand laying in the market, glass beneath his feet. What had he just done? There was no behavior bar alarm. This time it was a new alarm. A piercing alarm. It billowed throughout the whole city. Charlie looked across the town. Lights were flickering everywhere, and he could hear people screaming.

"Warning, warning, you have 360 minutes until a full town ReSet. Warning, Warning, You have 360 minutes until a full town ReSet." The alarm sounded over and over, and the behavior bar flashed a violent red at 100 percent. Picture-Perfect Charlie had just made his one and only mistake, and it could cost everyone their lives.

ONE SMALL PROBLEM

Charlie panicked and took off in a sprint. He had to get to the nearest safety entrance. He rounded the corner of the police station and saw the dumpster behind the library. He came to a halt and looked away immediately. No doubt Team Alpha was monitoring as their precious Utopian had just made it on the list of total obliteration and at the hand of their precious Charlie. He couldn't let them have any indication of what was going on. He knew that if his father's plan worked, they could not know where anyone was when they showed up to wipe them out. He knew his father's very first act was going to be to shut off everyone's chip if the alarm sounded, but Charlie's wasn't capable of that. He closed his eyes and held them closed tight. He extended his hands in front of him and began feeling in the cold dark night. He would have to do this step blindly.

Once he was underground and in his box, he could open his eyes again. At that moment, he was glad his father had made the town run drills at some of the entrance points. He was also grateful this was the easiest one. He knew he had to hurry; ten minutes wasn't very long. He finally felt the ice-cold hard steel under his hands. He knew the dumpster was flipped open on the industrial strength hinges. He bent down and got on his butt. He slowly scooted closer to where he believed the dumpster was. He had his left hand on the side of the dumpster and his right hand in front of him. He could tell he was at the opening. He sighed and scooted the rest of the way in.

He immediately felt his stomach drop and he knew he had made it in. He always got sick on the playground slide, and at every practice, he had gotten sick on this slide too. His body accelerated as the cold air hit him in the face. He could tell he was close to the landing. With a loud thud, his body hit the mats at the bottom of the dumpster slide, and he lay flat on his back, still not daring to open his eyes. He could hear utter chaos all around him as he managed to get to his feet. The voices were overlapping each other, and he couldn't pick them apart. He managed to get to the large dirt wall and find the railing the team had put together. He could hear the underground lights flickering above him. At least he had made it. He hoped everyone else had too. He felt a sharp pain in his stomach. He knew it wasn't the slide but rather the guilt and shame resulting from what he had done. It dawned on him; nobody knew yet. His father would be too busy getting everyone checked in to think about who caused the ReSet. He needed to get to his father. Suddenly, he felt a jolt against his stomach, and he fell hard to the ground, hearing a familiar voice.

"Charlie, oh heavens. I'm so sorry. Why do you have your eyes closed, dear?"

Charlie put a finger to his lips and tapped his heart twice. He knew she would know.

"Oh, yes. Of course, dear. Do you need help to your location?"

He nodded. Then, he pulled himself off the ground and extended his hand. Mrs. Treebler grabbed him by the hand and very briskly guided him. She, the town librarian, and Charlie had become fast friends when he was younger. He found the best way to occupy his time and stay out of trouble was to get lost in the adventures of all the books. Their library didn't have much of a selection, and he had read them all. Mrs. Treebler had grown very fond of Charlie, and once a month had started bringing him a book from her own private collection she had saved before the World ReOrder. He was so thankful she had made it. She was the eldest citizen, and he had been worried about her getting underground. She had joked that she was a tough old gal and told him not to worry. He was relieved that she was right. "We're here," she whispered. She lightly pushed Charlie inside, and he heard the slam of the door. He opened his eyes and the contrasting bright light caught him by surprise. He hadn't been underground since his father finished his box. There were air holes for breathing, and his dad had found a way to thin out the metal enough where it was semi-translucent and he could see out of it.

"Mrs. Treebler," he said. "Can you go tell my family I am where I should be and safe? Can you ask my father if there is anything I can do inside this thing, while I wait?"

"Sure thing, dear," she replied.

Charlie slumped in the corner. He couldn't believe this was happening. It had seemed like Mrs. Treebler had been gone for an eternity, although it was a mere hour. He was alarmed when she came back because she had a look of terror on her face.

***

Tommy sat up in his bed and looked out the window. He couldn't believe it. The city alarm was going off. He looked around his room. He was just lying there; he hadn't done anything. Why in the world was the alarm going off? His momma burst through the door.

"Oh, Tommy," she cried. "What did you do?"

He looked at her in horror. He shouldn't have been surprised that she expected him. Still, that was his momma; she could have at least asked.

"Momma," he pleaded. "I've just been lying here."

She shook her head in disgust and threw open his closet door.

"What are you doing, Momma?" he asked.

"I know you did something Thomas, and I'm going to find out what—not that it matters," she replied. "Grayson won't save us this time. All these people are going to die because of you."

She began sobbing loudly. Tommy felt his heart break. She didn't even know his secret, and yet she wouldn't look at him. There was a rapid knock on their front door. They both exchanged a quick glance and then she looked away again. Maybe the town was out there to take care of them personally. Tommy was beside himself; he really hadn't done anything. His mother left his room and came back within seconds with David King.

"Look, Tommy," he began. "I don't even want to hear it. You better be glad Mr. Newsome is a good man. You both need to come with me right now; we don't have much time."

David didn't leave them any time to ask questions. He turned and headed back out of their home. They didn't know what else to do, so they followed him. The night air was frigid, and a sense of dread billowed around them. The sound of the alarm blazed against their ears. David went right next door to their neighbor's house and opened it. The Tankersons followed, concerned as to what the neighbors would say about David's imposing behavior. To their surprise, the house was lit but there was no movement inside. Nobody running in to see who just barged through their door. The trio entered the master bedroom to find it a wreck. The closet door was open, and it was clear that the contents that were once in the closet were now occupying the floor. David went to the closet and knelt down. He removed a hatch and the floor opened up. He heard the faint gasps behind him but didn't stop. He turned to look at the Tankersons.

"You don't have a choice but to trust me. I'll explain it all once we're safe. You two go first, and I'll follow."

He stood up and pointed to the floor. He expected them to go in there. Tommy thought he had lost his mind. To his surprise, his mother went to the floor, sat down, scooted into the dark hole, and disappeared before his eyes. She hadn't even spoken to him or asked if he was okay. He was afraid he had lost his momma altogether. He had to do whatever he could to win her back. He had to convince her he didn't do anything this time. He made his way to the dark hole his mother had vanished into and jumped in.

When he came out the other side, he found himself in a dimly-lit corridor of sorts. The smell of dirt and steel engulfed his senses. He could hear chaos all around him, but since he hadn't bothered to spend any time with the town, he couldn't make any of the voices out. He didn't see his momma. She couldn't have gotten too far ahead. He decided to just follow the railing toward the voices. As he did, he passed several townspeople. He didn't know their names, but he recognized their faces. Unfortunately, this time, each face looked at him the exact same way. Each face was full of hate and rage. No doubt, they joined in with his mother in the assumption that he was the reason the city was in trouble. He had to find someone to listen to him. Then, he had an idea. He had to find Katie Newsome. Of all the people in the town, she had been the sincerest to him. Sure, Charlie had tried to "connect" with him, but he could feel it was always out of service. He could tell that Katie was genuine. He felt an overwhelming need to find Katie, as she could help him convince everyone. He knew he would need to find the Newsome family to find Katie. He also knew that this was throwing himself into the lion's den, but what other choice did he have? Katie was his only hope—his only chance.

He braved his way through more people and followed the noise as it increased. He turned a bend in the corridor and was caught off guard by what he saw. There was a huge open area with quad-stacked bunk beds attached to every wall, a large kitchen stocked with food, two sets of restrooms, and a large gathering of people. It seemed the whole town was there. Toward the front of the room was a small platform with a computer. Mr. and Mrs. Newsome were there, and so was his momma. Above the computer was a royal blue banner with gold lettering that read, "Undertopian: Staying Safe While No One is Watching." How in the world had this town created an entirely new town without him knowing? Had his mother known? Had she kept him from him? He didn't think so; she had seemed as shocked as he was when David King burst through the door. Mr. Newsome asked his momma something, and she dropped her head, but then nodded affirmatively. He assumed it was about him.

Tommy quickly scanned the crowd, looking for Katie. He wasn't paying attention at first, but then the whispers got louder. He looked up and realized that everyone was now staring at him. They were muttering about how he shouldn't get to be here. They were saying he should have been left to die. They did blame him. He shook his head no. He wanted to tell them it wasn't him, but he knew they wouldn't believe him. His heart began to race. He felt the sweat pouring from his temples. He slowly backed away. He needed to breathe. He didn't know what to do, but he had to get out of this great room. Mr. Newsome saw what was happening and knew he had to intervene. He took a step forward to gather everyone's attention. He began to direct the crowd back toward him. Tommy used this chance as a way to make his great escape. Maybe he should just hide for a bit and let everyone simmer until he could get to Katie.

***

It seemed as if Mrs. Treebler had been gone an incredibly long time. Charlie heard her calling his name before he even saw her. He could hear the trouble in her shaky voice. He stood to his feet to meet her gaze. By now, his parents would have everyone checked in. By now, all the secret passages would be forever sealed shut. By now, everyone would be on pins and needles waiting for the ReSet team to show up to destroy everyone. He knew they would all be bunkering down, holding their breath, hoping to never be found. Within the next hour, the full Alpha team should be above them wondering where everyone went. It was always Grayson's mission to do a full ReSet from time of alarm to completion in three hours. Mrs. Treebler was now in front of his box; she was out of breath and shaking violently.

"Mrs. Treebler," Charlie said. "What's wrong?"

"It's Katie," she said. "She is missing."

UNLIKELY DUO

Charlie scrambled back and slid down the wall landing hard on the floor. He could feel his heart rate increasing, and he knew he had to bring it down. He inhaled and exhaled slowly, his mind whirling with confusion. How could she be missing? She knew what to do. They had gone over it time and time again. Where was she? Had something happened to her? Was she just lost in the shuffle? Was she in the bathroom? He needed to go help find her. He had to gain his composure; he was useless the way he was acting now. He took another three breaths and slowly stood back up. He felt the earth shift around him, having stood up too fast. He walked over to the cot and sat down. He looked directly at Mrs. Treebler, trying to control his voice. The last thing he needed was Mrs. Treebler to get more worked up than she already was. He took a final breath.

"What do you mean missing?" he asked.

"We don't know," she said wearily. "Your mother is starting a grid search now. They were checking everyone off on the list, and Katie was the only one that didn't make roll. Your mother is in a panic. Your father is trying to be calm. He said she is probably just somewhere they haven't checked. Your mother doesn't agree. She said that Katie knew to go straight to the checkpoint. When they checked her chip, it was still showing that it was streaming, so your father manually shut it down. Since he can't view the feed, he couldn't tell where it was streaming from. Everyone is working on a search right now. Your father told me to tell you to just sit tight. He wanted to check in with your personally by now and try to start working on your chip, but the town needs him."

Charlie soaked in everything she said, periodically shaking his head in response. He knew in his bones that his mother was right. Katie did know better. She would have never skipped check-in. She would have never let her family worry like that. Where are you K.K.?

"Mrs. Treebler," he said. "You should probably get back to the search. Please tell my parents to let me know if I can do anything inside this box to help."

Mrs. Treebler was still muttering things under her breath, but she shook her head in compliance. As she walked away Charlie heard her say, "God forgive me, but I wish that Tankerson boy had never been born."

Charlie felt a ping of guilt run through his entire body. This time, it wasn't Tommy's fault. This one time. He couldn't believe he let his emotions get the best of him. He couldn't think about it. It didn't matter now. Tommy had ruined this town, and he was fine letting everyone think it was him. He convinced himself that it really was Tommy's fault. If Tommy hadn't climbed the bar so high, Charlie's one little mistake wouldn't have mattered. He knew the whole town would be understanding. He had never messed up; he deserved at least one mistake. He allowed his thought process to ease the guilt for the moment.

He shifted his focus back to his baby sister. He couldn't just sit there. He knew she had to be above ground. He was going to go find her. Then, it hit him. He knew how he could get around undetected. He had to get back to his house, without giving away his location on the feed that he knew Alpha was monitoring. He stopped for a moment relishing in the idea that Grayson Jeffers was probably so angry he was spitting fire. He had no way of knowing where an entire town had disappeared to.

Charlie had to be very careful to execute his plan flawlessly—otherwise, he would give away their location. He didn't intend on dooming the town twice. He scanned the room and saw a doodling journal and pencils on the makeshift desk in the corner. His father had come through yet again. He scribbled a quick note on the first page in the journal, left it open so it could be found, closed his eyes to shut off the feed, and headed out the door. He had blindly traveled this corridor once before and didn't do so well. As he opened his metal box and stepped out, he could hear the throngs of people shouting his sister's name in desperation. His heart sank. He knew they were wasting their time. He needed to move quickly to avoid being seen. He picked up his pace, feeling for the guardrail, heading away from the great room of Undertopian—away from all the people he loved. He had never felt lonelier than he did in that moment. The voices faded, and he knew he was close. His father had built a secret escape hatch that he had told nobody but Charlie, David, his mother, and himself about. He didn't want anyone getting worried about the plan and trying to leave prematurely. Charlie had the code and was going to use it. He knew as soon as he opened it, it would send off an alert to his father, so he would have to make his next move very quickly. The corridor had grown incredibly dark, so Charlie knew he was almost to the exit. He took another blind step and tripped, slamming his face into the dirt path. What had he just tripped on?

He reached out and, feeling a warm body, jumped back in surprise. He wanted desperately to open his eyes, but as dark as he knew this area was, it wouldn't have changed anything.

"Hey, at least buy me dinner before you go grabbing me like that."

Charlie was furious. Of course, Tommy Tankerson would somehow be in the way to ruin Charlie's plan to save Katie.

"Shut up Tommy," Charlie sneered. "I don't have time for your games. You need to go back the other way and not say anything."

"Oh, hey Picture-Perfect," he replied. "See, I knew you secretly..."

"I said shut up," Charlie nearly screamed.

This caught Tommy off guard. Charlie had never done anything so non-perfect before.

"Katie is missing, and I'm going to find her," Charlie finished.

Tommy did stop talking. He replayed in his head what Charlie had just said. Katie was missing. The Katie he was trying to find to help him. Tommy stood up from where he had been hiding. If she was missing, he was going to find her too. He didn't have a choice. He didn't stand a chance without her. "Okay," he said. "What's the plan?"

"Ha," Charlie laughed. "We're not going together. You and I don't work well together. I don't have time for your stupid behavior. I have to find my sister."

Charlie felt Tommy grab him by the shirt and pull him close. They were face to face. Charlie could feel Tommy's hot breath on his nose. Charlie balled his fists, ready to do whatever was necessary.

"It isn't a choice," Tommy snarled. "Believe it or not, Katie is important to me. I am going; I wasn't asking for your permission." He released Charlie and exhaled deeply.

Charlie could feel the tension lift as he began to speak again.

"I can't stay here, man; everyone hates me. I didn't make the mistake, though. I swear. Katie will believe me; she'll help me convince the town. My own momma doesn't love me anymore. I need Katie, and I'm going to help you. So, again, what's the plan?"

Charlie could hear the sadness in what Tommy said last. He knew there was no use fighting him. He could come, but he better stay out of his way.

"Fine," Charlie relented. "They can hear everything we're saying so from this point forward, don't talk to me. I don't want you to mess this up. I'll keep my eyes closed, so you need to be my eyes, okay?"

Charlie waited and Tommy didn't respond. Seriously, he was an idiot. "Okay?" Charlie asked again impatiently.

"You said not to talk, right?" Tommy asked.

Charlie huffed. This was going to be a disaster. He grabbed Tommy by the shirt and led him the rest of the way to the escape hatch. He ran his fingers down the wall until he felt what he was looking for. He finally felt the keypad and opened it up. He entered 5110, his parent's wedding anniversary backward, and heard the release of the hatch. He could feel the moonlight on his eyelids, and he crawled out. He could hear Tommy behind him. He closed the hatch, felt in the grass for the matching keypad, and entered the number again. He heard the hatch seal. They had done it; they had closed themselves off from the rest of the town—from their safety. He knew they were at the willow. He reached for Tommy, tapped him, and pointed up the hill. He hoped he was pointing to his house. Tommy opened Charlie's hand and tapped three times. "That means yes," he whispered. Irritated, Charlie shook his head. This boy really liked to bend all the rules, didn't he? He heard Tommy's footsteps in front of him accelerate, and Charlie joined him. The two ran silently up the hill. Charlie fell several times; this was not working. To his surprise, Tommy came back after the third fall, helped him up, grabbed the sleeve on his jersey, and practically pulled him up the hill.

Eventually, Charlie could tell they had reached the top of the hill. He slowed his steps and made it carefully to the door. He knew they had to beat the clock. The ReSet team would be showing up in droves of armored vehicles. Normally, they would be there to destroy the city, but not this time. He had no idea what Grayson's move would be, but he knew it would involve a search and likely destruction. That would be more out of anger than anything. Grayson Jeffers wasn't a man who liked to be bested, and this town had done it. Charlie loved that. He found the front door and opened it. He heard Tommy join him inside, and he shut it. He made his way to the kitchen and started opening drawers and feeling around. He wished he had paid a bit more attention when his mother put away groceries. By the time he had searched the sixth drawer, he let out an irritated sigh. This was taking too long.

"Just tell me what we need," Tommy interrupted.

Charlie was going to kill Tommy. He knew it. He told him, no talking. Charlie knew that Tommy was right; it would be easier for Tommy to find it and he was annoyed to admit it. "Aluminum foil," Charlie replied.

"Got it," Tommy said.

How had he found it so quickly? This just added to Charlie's annoyance. Then, he realized he would need his help again. He wasn't fond of relying on Tommy Tankerson.

"Wrap it around me," he said.

"Like a dress, Perfect?" Tommy mocked.

"Just do it, you buffoon," Charlie snapped.

He could tell Tommy was close to him, and he could hear the crinkling of the foil. Charlie lifted his arms as Tommy walked around him with the foil.

"Only around my chest, make sure to cover my heart," Charlie guided.

"There ya go ya, weirdo," Tommy replied after a few seconds. "You are officially the ugliest burrito I have ever seen."

Charlie opened his eyes and adjusted his sight. "You're a freaking idiot; did you know that?" Charlie said. "This foil is blocking the feed for the audio and visual of my chip. My father found a way to shut everyone else's off to keep our plan a secret, but mine is tricky. He hasn't figured it out yet. I had to have this foil to block the feed. I am going to have to keep reapplying, though, and I'm very limited in my movements."

"So, that's your big plan?" Tommy asked. "Wrap yourself up like food to go. That's as far as you got?"

"No," Charlie snapped. "Well, yes. Listen, I didn't have much time, and we're wasting time now. We just need to find my sister and get back to safety. I'll go back to my box, and my father will figure out the rest. Katie only has three places she would go, so I don't expect this to take very long. I'm going to check upstairs in her room, and then we'll go. See if you can find any more foil."

Charlie wasn't gone very long but came back empty-handed. He'd been hoping she would be hiding in the window seat bench their father had made her, but she wasn't. They had built a secret fort in the park across town, that was his next guess. He came into the living room and what he saw stopped him dead in his tracts. "Seriously?" he asked. Tommy had found a belt and had stuffed two boxes of aluminum foil on each hip. Stupider still, he had tied a dish rag around his head like some kind of ninja.

"Let's do this," he said.

Charlie wished he would take things more seriously. He walked to the door and opened it. It dawned on him that this would be the last time he would ever see this home again. Grayson would no doubt set fire to this one; it would be personal. Charlie looked over to the ornate entry table by the door. He had helped his father build it. It was the drop-off location for keys and miscellaneous items. On it, was a small, framed picture of his family on the opening day of Utopian. David had gifted it to them. His family looked so happy. He felt himself getting choked up. He grabbed the frame, got the picture out of it, and stuffed it into his pocket. They stepped out of the door and headed down the hill. They made it to the willow and heard a high-pitched scream. They both jumped behind the willow and crouched down, cupping their hands with their mouths.

"Let me go," she screamed.

Grayson emerged from behind the market holding Katie by the arms.

"Stop squirming and tell me where they are," he ordered.

Charlie felt fire deep inside him and he began to stand. The crinkling aluminum daring to give away his position. He didn't care. He felt a hard tug as Tommy pulled him back down. He turned to glare at him. Tommy shook his head and whispered. "You can't take him on yet. We have nothing to do it with. You can't help her like this."

He was right again. Charlie squatted back down, watching his sister in horror.

"I don't know," she cried.

"I don't believe that," Grayson replied. "Listen, Katie, you have always been my favorite Newsome. I mean that. You're thirteen now, and I think you understand how this works. I'm the boss. I'm in charge. You don't lie to me. There is no way an entire town disappears, and you don't know?" He condescendingly booped her nose.

Katie snapped at him, trying to bite his finger. "Listen, Jeffers," she replied coldly. "You've never been my favorite. Do you honestly think my family would have gone somewhere and left me? You found me hiding in the woods. Do you think if I knew where they were I would have been hiding in the woods? I was asleep when the alarm sounded. I had fallen asleep with my headphones on, which my father has told me not to do. When I finally woke up to the blaring alarm, my family was gone. I looked for them and couldn't find them. I got scared and ran to the woods. You can check the feed and that is what you'll see."

Charlie's heart sank. That's why she missed the checkpoint. Those stupid headphones. She missed the ten-minute deadline, and she knew it. She probably went to the woods, counting on her father shutting her feed off immediately. She knew she had to get far from the city for when they destroyed it. She didn't realize they didn't know she was missing until it was too late, and Grayson had already found her location.

"I'm still not buying it, little Newsome," Grayson replied. "That's fine. I'm trained at interrogation. We'll take this back to Alpha, and I'll get the information I need, one way or another. You hear me?" Grayson screamed into the dark night. "I have your daughter. I know you're here somewhere. I have her, and I'm taking her with me. You can't stop me, Newsome. You better just give up now if you want to see little Katie safe and sound. I am taking her. You know how to get in touch with me. I'm still sending my team, and we will find you. Do your daughter a favor and save us the trouble."

He was wrong. His father couldn't hear him at all. His father had no idea what was going on above ground.

"Please," Katie begged. "I don't know anything."

Grayson ignored her, grabbed her by the hair, and dragged her back toward the woods. "Let's go dear," he said. "Our chopper awaits."

SACRIFICE

Charlie and Tommy remained hidden behind the willow for what seemed like an eternity. They heard the whooshing of chopper blades far in the distance. The sound faded into the sky, and they watched in horror as the chopper flew above them, headed toward Alpha. His sister was in there, and he hadn't done anything to help her.

"Tommy," Charlie began.

"I know," Tommy said. He genuinely looked upset. "What do we need to do? I'm all in, but I'm doing this for Katie, not for you."

Charlie wondered why he was so set on helping Katie. Tommy didn't care about anyone but himself. It didn't matter, though. They had to move quickly. They had to get out of this town before the ReSetters showed up. He didn't waste time discussing the plan with Tommy. He took off at a dead sprint back up the hill. He had to get to the car. They had to go to Phoenix. They needed a safe place, supplies, weapons, and somewhere for Charlie to come up with a plan. Staying in Utopian was sure to get them killed. He heard Tommy following behind him. They made it back to the house and Charlie heard his aluminum tear. He looked down and there was a rip in the side. They stopped to reapply, and then Charlie made his way to the car. He convinced himself that driving a car was surely like driving a go-cart and it would be a piece of cake.

"Nice," Tommy said. "We've got wheels. Now step aside and let me handle this. My dad had magazines on cars and engines and stuff like that. I can figure out how to hotwire this thing in no time." He cracked his knuckles and opened the driver's-side door.

Charlie stepped away as Tommy started using a pair of nail clippers he had found in the car to try and remove the portion under the steering wheel column.

"Tommy," Charlie began.

"Don't interrupt me Picture-Perfect," he said. "Let me do this. You aren't the only one who can come up with a plan. I'm working with what I've got. Give me like ten minutes. I swear."

"Or," Charlie replied, "we could go now."

Tommy looked back to see Charlie dangling a set of car keys. Tommy felt his face grow red. Why did Charlie always have to be so perfect? He wanted to argue out of spite, but then he thought of how terrified Katie had looked and chose to not waste the time. He got up from the ground, jumped into the passenger seat, and looked patiently at Charlie. Charlie got in, cranked the car, and slowly backed down the driveway.

Before too long, they were on their way to Phoenix. Tommy hadn't let up about where they were going, so Charlie finally told him.

Tommy felt sick to his stomach. They were going to the town he had destroyed. There was also a secret that had been haunting Tommy from that town, and he wasn't ready to face it again. Yet, Charlie argued with Tommy that there was no other way, and Tommy knew Charlie was right. He hated that he was right. They drove the entire trip in complete silence. They only stopped once to use the restroom on the side of the road and re-apply the foil. Charlie knew that the foil wasn't going to be a lasting solution. He focused the rest of the trip, trying to come up with a more permanent solution. They finally rolled into Phoenix. It was early in the morning, and Charlie was exhausted. On the last leg of the trip, he had felt his eyes getting heavy. He was surprised that Tommy stayed awake the entire trip. They didn't speak, but he got the sense that he was staying awake for Charlie's sake. Which wouldn't make any sense, given Tommy's self-centered nature. They passed the Phoenix sign, which was in the same terrible state that Charlie remembered from their trip almost a year ago.

"Stop the car," Tommy yelled.

Charlie halted the car with a hard break, slamming both of the boys forward into the dash and steering wheel. He quickly checked around him, wondering what Tommy saw that terrified him so much.

"I can't do it, man. I can't be back here," Tommy said.

Charlie didn't have time for this. By now, the ReSetters would be tearing apart his beloved city, looking for all the people he cared about. By now, Grayson would be doing who knows what to his kid sister, and by now, his family would have realized that he, too, was missing. He didn't have time to deal with Tommy chickening out.

"You can and you will," Charlie said.

"No, I really can't. You're on your own, pal. I can't do this," he replied. He visually looked as if he had seen a ghost.

Charlie was over it; he was over Tommy Tankerson. "You are worthless," Charlie replied. "Do you only ever think of yourself? You suddenly are too good to help someone. Do you understand that you are the reason my sister is gone? You are the reason our whole town had to build a secret town in the first place? Have you not stopped to wonder why nobody told you and your momma? We don't trust you. You were only saved because my father is too good of a man. If it were up to the rest of the town, I promise you would have been left for Grayson with a bow on your head. I'm sick and tired of dealing with you and your selfishness. For once in your life, stop thinking ..."

"I killed my papa," Tommy blurted out. Then, Tommy did something Charlie had never seen before. He began sobbing. Big ugly tears fell into his lap. Charlie opened his mouth to speak but didn't know what to say. Had he heard him correctly? Embarrassed, Tommy blew his nose into his sleeve and tried to clean up his face.

He hadn't meant to ever tell anyone his secret, especially not the one person he despised the most. He could feel Charlie staring at him in disbelief. He knew he would have to give the details.

"Not intentionally," Tommy began. "You see I love my papa more than anything in this world. He was an incredible man, husband, and father. I worshipped him. He was the law enforcement of the town, so much like you, I was perfect. I was the Picture-Perfect of my town. Unlike you, I couldn't handle the pressure. I snapped. It had only been like four months or something, and I was itching to just do something. I didn't even want to do something bad; I just wanted to do something fun. It started with little things at school. Then I wanted to do more. I learned how to trick my device. One evening, I went to one of our neighbors' houses and I got her cat and its leash out of her garage. I also thought it was so stupid that Mrs. Jenkins walked her cat on a leash. Who does that? Anyway, I climbed up a tree, put the cat up there, and tied the leash to one of the branches. I was going to get the cat down. It was just a small prank. The behavior bar chimed, and I felt accomplished. I had gotten my first mark for something other than pulling a pigtail. I knew I would have to answer to it from my papa and Mr. Bo, but it was worth it to me. I walked away to go shoot some hoops, hoping my neighbor would get a little panicky. Then, I would come back, get that stupid cat, and look like a hero. I lost track of time playing basketball. It began to rain and I knew that cat would be having a fit trying to get down. I didn't want it to hang itself or something like that, so I ran back to rescue it. When I turned the corner, I saw my papa on a ladder already trying to get it out of the tree. He unhooked the leash and was on his way down. I slowed my steps and figured I would just casually walk up to him. I wasn't ready to come clean yet. He was at the top of the ladder and a thunder cloud boomed and lightning snapped. The cat got scared and scratched, trying to get away from the storm. It got my dad in the face and because of the rain, he lost his footing on the ladder. I saw him falling; it was almost in slow motion. I ran as fast as I could, screaming to him. I didn't get there in time. He fell and slammed his head on the concrete. I made it to him and collapsed. I tried to stop the bleeding; I swear I tried. There was so much ... so much blood. I yelled for him to wake up, but he didn't."

Tommy stopped speaking and began sobbing again. He pulled his knees close to his chest, held them tight, and just wept.

Charlie listened silently. He couldn't believe that Tommy had been carrying this secret around with him. He understood why he felt the need to keep it quiet. He didn't know what to say to comfort Tommy. They had been enemies for so long that he wasn't sure how to be a friend to him. Charlie felt the sting of guilt and pain forming in the pit of his stomach.

Through his knees, Tommy began to speak again. "I killed him. If I hadn't decided to be bad, then none of this would have happened. It was one mistake. After that, I lost it, man. The secret was eating me alive. I didn't know how to escape. I lived every day wondering when someone would find out. I had learned how to trick my feed, so I knew the Alpha team had no idea. Honestly, I was kinda hoping that if I was the reason for all the bad that maybe Grayson would just take me out. I wanted to be good again, but I felt like a didn't deserve a happy life, not after what I did."

"Tommy," Charlie began. "I'm so sorry that happened. I know why you think you're to blame, but a freak accident took your father's life, not you."

"Please don't try to empathize," he replied. "You have never done what I have done. You can't possibly understand how I feel."

"I caused the ReSet," Charlie quietly admitted. "I made the final mistake that sent Utopian underground. I threw a rock, and it shattered a window. I didn't even realize I was doing it until it was too late. Now, my sister has been kidnapped and everyone I love is underground, hiding, fearing for their lives. So, it may not be the same, but yeah, I get it, okay? There's nothing we can do to go back, Tommy. We have to move forward. We have to act now and set things right. Both of us owe it to everyone to do this. We owe it to Katie. I don't know why you're so set on helping her, but I know you are. So let's see this through. I came up with a plan on the way here. You still in?"

Tommy slowly looked up from his knees. He opened Charlie's hand and tapped three times. Charlie pushed his hand away but both boys looked at each other. For the first time, it wasn't with disdain. They had just shared their darkest secrets. They had related in a way no one else could. Without speaking, it seemed as if they had just formed a pact. An alliance forged through pain and brokenness. An alliance like that is hard to break.

Charlie put the car back in drive and headed to the doctor's office. He quickly ran inside, grabbed what he thought he would need, and headed down the road. They traveled toward the end of town and ditched the car in the woods, hiding it. Then, they made their way to Bo's place on foot. It had been a while since Charlie had been there. Once inside, Charlie made his way to the kitchen.

"So," Tommy began. "What's the plan?"

"You're not going to like it," Charlie said.

Charlie spent the next hour explaining exactly what they needed to do. Tommy didn't like it. He kept telling Charlie he couldn't do it. He kept telling Charlie they had to find another way. Charlie urged Tommy to listen to what he was saying. There was no other way. There was no time. It was their only chance. Charlie had gone over it time and time again. He didn't waste any more time arguing with Tommy. He went to Bo's office and got on the computer. He needed to get two messages out before he did this. After he made it into Bo's office alone, he sat at the computer for several minutes. It was a stupid plan. He wasn't actually sure it would work. He told Tommy that no matter what, he had to continue. Help Katie. Get back to his father. Stay alive and save the world. That's what he kept telling Tommy. Charlie couldn't help smiling at the cruel irony that the fate of their futures came down to Tommy and Charlie, working together—as partners. He couldn't say that he liked Tommy, but he did understand a little more how everything came to be. He couldn't imagine living with the pain of ending his father's life. He used his father's hack codes and got into the Alpha monitoring lists. He embedded a message into the Utopian one. He knew his dad would get the alert and understand.

"Me and Tank safe. Have a Plan. Will hurry back. Stay Put. G.J. took K.K. Working on it. Love you more than you will ever know, Champ."

It was hard for him to write the last part. He felt the hard lump in his throat. He knew that may very well be the last thing he ever got to write or say to his father. He wished he could elaborate on how lucky he was to have lived being his son. A tear fell on the keyboard, and Charlie knew he had to snap out of it. His sister needed him. The next message was to Bo at Alpha. He knew that Bo and Heathrow were working from the inside. This email would go to a private backdoor Bo had set up.

"Keep her safe. We have a plan. Bringing a team. Be there as soon as we can. Be Ready."

Okay. There was nothing left to do except the one thing he didn't want to: finish his plan. He walked back to the kitchen and Tommy was still sitting where he left him. He looked green in the face. Tommy looked at him and Charlie could see the fear in his eyes.

"I can't man," Tommy said. "Please don't make me. I just can't."

Charlie mouthed that he was sorry and slowly took the aluminum foil off. The entire time Tommy shook his head no. It didn't matter. This was the only way. The foil was completely off. Charlie counted to ten in his head. He knew the team would be picking the feedback up and getting Grayson's attention. He needed to make sure there was a full audience. He hoped that Katie wasn't watching.

"You're pathetic," Charlie began. "I can't believe you did this to our town. I'm so sick and tired of you. This is my town. I love Utopian. You don't. You don't care about anyone but yourself."

Charlie was trying hard to antagonize Tommy, but he could tell it wasn't working. Tommy was just sitting there. Charlie mouthed to Tommy, "please, for Katie." He still saw the hesitation, but that seemed to do the trick.

"Shut up Picture-Perfect," he replied. "I'm so sick of you being so high and mighty. You think you can't do anything wrong. I wish you weren't even here." His delivery wasn't as hateful as it should have been, but at least he was cooperating. Charlie knew he needed to escalate things quickly. If the feed was on too long, they would realize they weren't at Utopian at all. Even with the lights off in the house, the dim morning light from the windows would give enough away if they didn't hurry.

"You think you can do something about it," barked Charlie, giving Tommy a push. "You're just a bully. You're all talk and no action. I'm sick and tired of your mouth. What do we have to lose? Everything is ruined because of you. You want to fight me? Let's go. It is about time somebody taught you a lesson."

Charlie approached Tommy and punched him hard in the lip. Tommy began to bleed. Charlie's eyes widened with surprise. He hadn't meant to hit him that hard, but it had to be believable. Tommy pushed him back. Charlie pushed again. This time pinning him against the island in the kitchen.

"You know what, Tommy," he said. "It's a good thing your dad isn't alive, or he would be just as disgusted with you as everyone else in our town." Charlie hated to say it. He didn't mean it. He didn't want to hurt Tommy all over again. He looked at Tommy as the pain spread across his face. Even after saying that, he could tell Tommy didn't want to follow through.

"Tommy," Charlie screamed. "You think you can do something. I just proved you wrong. You are nothing! You will never be anything, and I dare you to try."

Tommy closed his eyes. He held them shut for a few seconds. Then, he began to scream at the top of his lungs. He grabbed a knife from the chopping block and charged Charlie.

Charlie saw it in his eyes. He saw the despair. Charlie was so afraid. He put his hands up and told Tommy to stop. He felt the blade plunge into his chest. His throat made a gurgling sound as he tasted the hot copper blood in his mouth. He dropped to his knees and looked deep into Tommy's eyes. Tommy was crying and saying he was sorry. Charlie fell to his back and thought of his family. A single tear rolled down his left eye as both eyes slowly closed. He felt a cold chill and could hear Tommy sobbing. Everything began to grow dark. He gasped and grabbed the knife as his heart stopped.

ABOUT THE AUTHOR

Savanna Loy is a debut author and writes across multiple genres. Her love for writing started when she had vivid dreams about the stories and plots which now have taken life in the form of her books.

She is a Texas native who is married to her RN husband, and together they are raising six kiddos ages eight and under (yes you read that correct!) five of which are foster kids whom they have adopted. She is also a breeder of bernedoodles.

She runs on coffee and Jesus ☺.

It was her childhood dream to become an author and she is excited to begin this part of her life by fulfilling her dream of being an author and creating worlds of escape for people everywhere.

You can follow her journey at *www.authorsavyloy.com*

UPCOMING

Children's Book

Releasing This Christmas

Made in the USA
Monee, IL
24 March 2023